Ragtop DOLL ©

Ragtop DOLL ©

THE SHOCKING AND HERETOFORE UNTOLD
ACCOUNT OF HOW MURDER, SEX AND
HARDBALL POLITICS STAINED AMERICA'S
1968 PRESIDENTIAL ELECTION

A STORY BY

RICH HALLADAY

Harmonie Park Press
Sterling Heights, Michigan

The story *Ragtop Doll©* is entirely a work of fiction.

In this work of fiction, names, characters, places, and incidents either are the product of the author's imagination or are used fictitiously. Any resemblance to actual organizations, business establishments, products, events, locales, or persons, living or dead, are imagined by the reader and/or are entirely coincidental.

The fact that names of some real persons, living or dead, are mentioned in the novel should not be construed as their having had involvement in the fictitious events portrayed.

The publisher does not have any control over, and does not assume any responsibility for, author or third party websites or their content.

Printed and bound in the United States of America

Published by
Harmonie Park Press
Liberty Professional Center
35675 Mound Road
Sterling Heights, MI 48310-4727
www.harmonieparkpress.com

Cover design:
Peri Poloni-Gabriel, Knockout Design, www.knockoutbooks.com

ISBN: 0-89990-153-0
ISBN 13: 978-0-899901-53-4

Library of Congress Cataloging-in-Publication Data

Halladay, Rich, 1937–
    Ragtop doll : the shocking and heretofore untold account of how murder, sex and hardball politics stained America's 1968 presidential election : a story / by Rich Halladay.
        p. cm.
    ISBN 0-89990-153-0 (alk. paper)
    1. Presidents—United States—Election—1968—Fiction. 2. United States—Politics and government—1963–1969—Fiction. 3. Kennedy, Robert F., 1925–1968—Fiction. 4. Political fiction. I. Title.
    PS3608.A548245R34 2010
    813'.6—dc22

                                                        2010035722

Ragtop Doll© is dedicated to Karin Marie-Ann,
Malin Kristina, Sara Viveka, and Anika Hillevi

May each of these exceedingly vibrant women
continue to live full, giving, and artful lives
while sharing their brains, beauty, and bounty
with those whom they choose to love

◄ Contents ►

Epilogue

Postscript

◄ Acknowledgments ►

The author wishes to thank the following, among many, who have provided inspiration, encouragement, stimulation, and/or counsel regarding development, writing, and publication of my story *Ragtop Doll©*:

Margareta Andén, Sven Andén, Hans Bagner, Armand Blinki, Andrea Bocelli, Darlene Brown, John Campbell, Chevrolet Motor Division, Eric Fris, Dave Gorzelski, Andrew Haley Jr., Austin Hill, Hubert Humphrey Jr., Harley-Davidson, Darlene Jankowski, Joe Kohler, Lili-Ann Ledin, Colleen McRorie, Brittmarie Särnö, Karen Simmons, Kyle Smith, John Telford, Harry Treleavan, Richard Wise, Marian Villerot Zander, Ron Ziegler, Katharine Zuckerman, and Marvin Zuckerman.

"In real life, unlike in Shakespeare, the sweetness of the rose depends upon the name it bears. Things are not only what they are. They are, in very important respects, what they seem to be."

HUBERT HUMPHREY
Vice President of the United States
under President Lyndon B. Johnson,
January 20, 1965–January 20, 1969

‹ P r o l o g u e ›

Bad Axe, Michigan, U.S.A.:
A Wednesday Afternoon in November 1996

It's a little after three o'clock on a mid-November afternoon, and the diffused sunlight makes the few cloud puffs seem pasted onto an otherwise crystal-clear Swedish-blue kind of sky.

A highly polished 1960s-era bright red Camaro convertible with a 350 V-8 and red-line tires roars to life. Seemingly incongruous for a chilly November day, the car's ragtop is folded down, revealing three occupants bundled up against the cold— a woman and two men of indeterminate ages.

Pulling away from the curb in front of the Huron County Court House, the classic Chevy moves slowly west along Huron Avenue in the undistinguished downtown of Bad Axe, the Huron County seat located in the center of Michigan's distinctively shaped Thumb area.

The stark, almost motionless small-town scene mirrors the hundreds—no, thousands—of other grey one-stoplight *Dullvilles* that dot America's landscape.

Except for two nasty-looking pickups and a shiny new Huron County sheriff's Ford patrol car, the only traffic on Huron Avenue is pedestrian. Across the street, two senior citizens are toting their groceries home in colorful cloth bags provided free as a sales incentive by the only grocery store still doing business downtown.

Brand-new Wal-Mart, Farmer Jack, and Kmart stores—built on fertile cropland along the north edge of town, just across from a McDonald's and several other high-calorific competitors on Fast Food Row—have siphoned most of the business away from the rich variety of shops that had operated and thrived for over a century downtown along both sides of Huron Avenue.

The few merchants remaining downtown continue to accuse and lambaste the deep-pocketed retail giants of using artificially low prices as a business tactic. The local *Bad Axe Hatchet* newspaper refused to support downtown merchants in any way when the new stores on the north side of town threatened to stop advertising in the paper, so the downtown stores were reduced to using weekly promotional flyers delivered by mail.

The giant chain stores—especially the Wal-Mart behemoth—countered with a flurry of fancy, high-priced press releases saying large retailers were simply exercising their God-given right to practice American free enterprise. They claimed to be doing a favor for consumers throughout Huron County by offering one-stop shopping and lower prices. And, after all, it's a tough argument to counter, except for all the poor folks in the area who contend they are being overcharged for lesser-quality food and merchandise. And, then there are the Wal-Mart employees who complain they are underpaid and lack commonplace company benefits! Many folks nowadays tend to believe that life in Bad Axe is increasingly raw and unfair!

Many mature area residents think the *Bad Axe Hatchet* has become an extension of the new retailers' huge corporate public relations and advertising departments. While the newspaper's publisher, Wayne Hogen, depends upon the big-box retail advertisers to provide important income, his wife, editor Ardell Hogen, knows she can fill space with an almost nonstop supply of self-serving press releases. The Hogens' business and editorial model definitely seems more in tune with William Randolph

Hearst than Andrew Greeley!

As Wal-Mart's top management in far away Arkansas moves inexorably toward fulfilling Sam Walton's dream of becoming America's largest business enterprise, the remaining small and marginal retailers in Bad Axe—and in towns like it all across America—slowly twist in the wind before they wither and die. Every small retail business owner in Bad Axe knows it's only a matter of time before he or she will be posting *de rigueur* red and white "OUT OF BUSINESS" signs in their front windows. It's a phenomenon that's become a uniquely American conundrum.

As the traffic light turns green, the red Chevy ragtop—a very special automobile because it was originally given to a friend almost thirty years ago as a gift by the then sitting vice president of the United States—swings left onto South Port Crescent and disappears just short of Murphy's Bakery & Coffee Shop.

Reaching America's East Coast in two days, by driving south to Toledo and turning left, this wonderful vintage convertible will be driven to New Haven, Connecticut, and loaded aboard the giant, but now empty Swedish cargo ship, the S.S. *Saab*, for the final leg of its improbable journey across the Atlantic Ocean— from Bad Axe, Michigan to Fiskebäckskil, the historic fishing village on Skaftö Island in West Sweden.

◄ Chapter 1 ►

Hunkered Down in a Huron County Michigan Jail Cell,
Alec Ramsay Ponders Suicide

THURSDAY, FEBRUARY 1, 1996

A large bronze plaque dedicated to U.S. President Richard Nixon is screwed permanently into the grey granite wall just to the right of the oversized front entrance double doors of the Huron County Building in Bad Axe, Michigan. The building, which faces north onto Huron Avenue, houses the county jail, a courtroom and various county departments.

In one-inch raised lettering, the plaque states in plain, unpunctuated English:

RICHARD M. NIXON

37TH PRESIDENT

OF THE

UNITED STATES

ON APRIL 10, 1974

AND ON THIS SPOT

MADE HIS LAST CAMPAIGN

APPEARANCE AS PRESIDENT

Less than a hundred feet away, sitting on the edge of his sparse jailhouse cot covered by a soiled threadbare blanket, a sullen Alexander Ramsay contemplates suicide. Townsfolk call it the "Big S."

Ramsay is celebrating one month of solitary incarceration in an 8 x 10-foot windowless cell tucked at the butt end of a third floor hallway.

Ramsay's life has turned to shit. Isn't it a shame to see such a dramatic downshift in the life of a fellow whose friends mostly thought him to be a solid model for good humor and old-fashioned optimism?

After all, wasn't he a guy whom President Richard Nixon's chief of staff, Bob Haldeman, had invited to join the White House communications staff following the epic 1968 presidential election battle and Nixon's victory against former U.S. Vice President Hubert Horatio Humphrey?

Some say Ramsay's problems can be traced to his refusal to budge, even a smidgeon, with regard to a lingering and ugly family probate matter. Furthermore, he won't deny nor comment upon an allegation that he threatened his sister's schlock lawyer, Morgan Childress, with some rather imaginative bodily harm.

Particularly galling to Ramsay is the fact that his sister's lawyer had quietly arranged to sell the Ramsays' centennial family farm to a close political ally who just happens to be the local probate judge handling Ramsay's parents' estate. The farm, which had been in the Richmond-Ramsay family since the early 1830s, is alleged to have been sold without permission, proper notice nor legal recourse.

The selling price of the main house, three large connected barns, and one hundred tillable acres was a ridiculously low $279,000 . . . estimated by Ramsay to be one third to one quarter of the property's true market value at the time. Only Ramsay's estranged sister and her shyster lawyer-friend know where the money went, although Alec Ramsay believes that the dough was probably split about evenly between their respective bank accounts.

He certainly didn't see any of it!

During his one month in jail, Ramsay's light brown-tinted hair has started to give way to the silvery-white crown that he has kept hidden for many years. Just a short time in Huron County's jail seems light years away from longtime barber Bill DeLosch, owner of Mr. D's Barbershop in Bloomfield Hills. It was DeLosch who had carefully tended to Ramsay's hair monthly for almost twenty-five years.

———

Ramsay has just pounded out these words on a circa-1912 L.C. Smith typewriter: "Today, February 1, 1996, my dad, Eric Richmond Ramsay, would have been ninety-two years old. I'm sure glad he's dead and unable to see me rotting away in this Huron County hellhole. It would have killed him!"

Aside from Ramsay's antique typewriter, for which the sheriff grudgingly granted a special concession because of Ramsay's modicum of local celebrity, the only personal items in the cell are Ramsay's small black leather 1996 Franklin Planner, a stack of yellow legal-size writing pads, two boxes of yellow Papermate #2 Sharpwriters, a few 9 x 12-inch grey envelopes taken years before from J. Walter Thompson in Manhattan, and three small color photos stuck on the wall with toothpaste.

One picture shows a bright red 1968 Camaro RS/SS convertible with a white top and an attractive blonde standing next to it. The second photo is of a white-columned Greek Revival-style farmhouse set atop a large grassy knoll ringed with green-turning-yellow-and-orange maples and what is reputed to be Michigan's largest black walnut tree.

Yet another picture is actually five taped-together snapshots that form a panoramic view of Ramsay's favorite place in the world, a historic and picturesque Swedish west coast fishing village named Fiskebäckskil, located on the island of Skaftö north of Göteborg. Göteborg [some say Gothenburg] is Sweden's second largest city, after Stockholm.

Ramsay's personal attributes churn in his mind as he paces the tiny cell and mumbles almost inaudibly to himself: "Fucking-A! Look at me. What's left? Late fiftyish. Still visible on my throat after all these years is a God-damned wicked-looking scar caused many years ago when an out-of-control yellow McCullagh chain saw chewed up the flesh while I trimmed trees in the Ann Arbor backyard of my favorite University of Michigan teacher, Professor Douglas Crary."

Alec Ramsay was twenty-two and remembers having to drive himself to the U of M Hospital's emergency entrance after his tree maintenance partner, a strapping Albion College football starting quarterback, earned Ramsay's enmity when he fainted from the sight of blood spewing from Ramsay's throat.

———

Tinted gold-rimmed Bausch & Lomb aviator-style eyeglasses adorn Ramsay's clean-shaven face. The thirty-three-year-old Rolex GMT-Master on his right wrist was bought new while Ramsay worked at J. Walter Thompson Company's headquarters in Manhattan during the '60s. Rolex was one among many of the company's blue-chip clients.

Perhaps of less merit was Ramsay's successful bid to avoid serving in America's Vietnam misadventure. After sensing that he might soon be called to active military duty, Ramsay did some informal research and succeeded in manipulating a rather disorganized U.S. military system. He thus avoided the possibility of service in Vietnam by joining the Michigan National Guard, an even more backward operation.

Ramsay spent one miserably cold and snowy late winter slogging through the U.S. Army's basic training course at Missouri's bleak Fort Leonard Wood. That was followed by an almost idyllic spring and summer in at the U.S. Army Signal School at Fort Monmouth, New Jersey.

Nearly every guy stationed at Fort Monmouth had a car. Ramsay's was the same dark green 1951 Chevy coupé that he had used while attending the University of Michigan, and for two cross-country jaunts between Michigan and California during his late teens.

Back in 1961, Fort Monmouth was known as the "Country Club of the Army" because of its unmatched facilities and staff, and the high quality of its specialized programs and student-soldiers. Maybe best of all, Fort Monmouth wasn't tucked away in some out-of-the-way hick state where ignorant natives spoke incoherently with a drawl and too often claimed to be reborn in the image of Christ.

Fort Monmouth offered another attractive advantage: Wide, warm, sandy Atlantic beaches where Ramsay often went alone to body surf and lie on the beach. New Jersey locals were too smart to claim their Atlantic waves were better than the pounding Malibu surf that Ramsay loved so much. There, nothing matched the exhilaration of "hanging ten" on a longboard before, all too frequently, wiping out just short of the beach.

Although Spec-4 Ramsay's military M.O.S. required that he be assigned a .45-caliber automatic pistol rather than a rifle, this hip-pocket pacifist from Michigan took considerable pride in knowing that he had actually out-shot for record every gun-toting cowboy and loudmouth braggadocio hunter—from Oklahoma, both Dakotas and Alaska—who were stationed with him at Fort Leonard Wood.

Ramsay attributed his skill with weapons—the .45 pistol, a carbine and M-16 rifle—to his good listening skills. Plus, the weapons instructors at Fort Leonard Wood were as good as the army's food was bad!

In the creases and recesses of his mind, Ramsay realized that if things turned really sour, his shooting skills would make him a prime candidate for the infantry. But that was not his game plan. Indeed, Ramsay had joined the Guard only after receiving a written document promising he would be trained to shoot still-photography and movies, not guns.

Aside from following instructions from his military instructors, maybe Ramsay's otherwise unexplained prowess with weapons resulted from the light brown-tinted prescription eyeglasses he obtained at Fort Leonard Wood. They were prescribed by a sympathetic army doctor as an antidote to Ramsay's real or imag-ined symptoms for snow blindness during that cold Missouri winter. The young soldier developed his own long weapons' aiming system by learning to rest his right thumb against the clear plastic eyeglass frame.

In any case, the tinted eyeglasses Ramsay wore everywhere became his military trademark.

To hard-nosed superiors at both Fort Leonard Wood and Fort Monmouth, Ramsay's distinctive eyewear was a constant "red flag" and a reminder that Ramsay was a different kind of American soldier.

Whenever a fresh superior officer shouted "Hey, soldier, sunglasses aren't permitted here. Get them off," Ramsay reached into his pocket and produced the original handwritten and dog-eared prescription signed by Major Dr. Ed Wilson at Fort Leonard Wood. As a precaution, Ramsay kept three copies of the precious eyeglass prescription at the bottom in his duffel bag. Another copy had been mailed home for safekeeping.

Alec Ramsay, the mock soldier disguised as a Michigan National Guardsman, never was bothered much by the usual military minutia, bullshit and chain-of-command issues. Carefully walking along the edge of military regulations, he just wanted to successfully complete the much-coveted still photography and motion picture photography double curricula at Fort Monmouth, and then get on with his life while others fought Lyndon Johnson's stupid, deadly and unwinnable war in Vietnam.

Evidently one of Ramsay's motion picture instructors, Frank Capra, Jr., had reached pretty much the same conclusion. Although young Capra grew up alongside the Pacific Ocean near Los Angeles, he told Ramsay that surfing was never his gig. Capra drew himself erect as he declared, "Me? I'm a sailing man!"

Capra compensated for his lack of will and skill to pilot a surfboard by learning to sail his family's West Sweden-built sailboat. The forty-five-foot craft was kept in the marina at Red Bank, not too far north of the Fort Monmouth campus. And young Frank helped assure continuation of his sailing pleasures by periodically hosting Fort Monmouth's admiring and too-pliable military brass.

———

In his early teens, long before embarking on his abbreviated faux military career, Ramsay earned the rank of Eagle Scout in Detroit's Boy Scout Troop 211. As a Boy Scout, he had been honored to help lead the large Detroit contingent to the 1953

Boy Scout World Jamboree at the Irvine Ranch in Orange County, California.

He also served two years as captain of the safety patrol at Detroit's Issac Crary Elementary school, on the corner of Puritan and Asbury Park. At the time, it seemed like a really big deal because Ramsay got to attend the city's safety patrol summer camp. That's where he was able to meet the likes of Detroit Tigers left-handed pitcher Ted Gray and Officer Thad Kitchen of the Detroit Police Department, who was handler of a champion German Shepard jumper named Safety Girl of Detroit.

Ramsay was particularly proud, during his junior year in high school, to have been elected president of Cooley High's National Honor Society chapter. According to close friends, this was an event that for some years afterward continued to piss off Ramsay's main challenger for his school's NHS leadership role— a good-looking blond, smart-as-a-whip, multi-talented and person- able lad named Jimmy Olesen.

Four-and-a-half years at The University of Michigan and, later on, some graduate-level marketing and finance courses at Harvard and Wharton would provide a counterpoint to the fact that Ramsay had dropped out of law school after one semester. Maybe that's when he acquired the seed to his persistent loathing for America's lawyer class!

―――――

A happy irony suddenly races through Ramsay's secular, clearly non-religious mind. In 1957, he wore Metropolitan Opera legend Richard Crooks' white, tinged-with-burgundy choir robe while singing in the choir every Sunday morning at All Saints' Episcopal Church on Camden Drive at Santa Monica Boulevard in Beverly

Hills, California. It was All Saints' that helped provide Ramsay with a semblance of social life in California. He did lots of fun things, like arranging for church member Fred Astaire to visit one Thursday evening to regale girls and boys in the St. Christopher's Youth Group about his love of the dance. Which young lady there could resist a chance to twirl around the floor with Mr. Astaire? Maybe one or two of them might like to know better the young fellow from Michigan who made it possible? Ramsay also enjoyed meeting church members like Lauren Bacall, Jayne Mansfield and her live-in boyfriend-soon-to-be-husband, a former Mr. Universe from Hungary, named Mickey Hargitay.

The irony is that, in 1968, Ramsay married the lovely Marie-Ann Eklund, a Swedish lass from Göteborg, in a wonderfully low-key ceremony at another All Saints' Episcopal Church—this one located on East 60th Street in Manhattan.

Curiously, both Marie-Ann and Alec were then, and have remained, secularists. But the church was conveniently located next to their apartment building at 220 East 60th. And after all, they reasoned, who wants to travel any farther than necessary when you're madly in love and frothing to marry?

————

Constantly pulsing through Ramsay's mind is the possibility that he is afflicted with Tourrette's Syndrome. This belief seems to be reinforced by the fact that the phrase "Fucking-A" all too frequently spills uncontrollably from his lips. The condition offers the increasingly unbalanced Ramsay yet another reason to end his life tonight by doing a *neck dangle* from his cell's uppermost cold-rolled steel crossbar!

———

Now, almost trance like, the names of four special women in his life tumble from Ramsay's mouth. There's perky Kalifornia Katherine in Southern California, the tiny dark-haired and dark-eyed surfer girl with whom Ramsay has stayed in-touch since 1957.

They met in California when she was sixteen, soon after Ramsay saw her featured in a *Life* magazine article about her father's new book, entitled *Gidget*, which was written to document his daughter's surfing adventures. Already a university student in Ann Arbor, Ramsay decided to skip school for a year so he could drive his 1951 dark green Chevy to California, where—at least in his mind—he found Katherine waiting for him. He sometimes called her K.K., shorthand for Kalifornia Katherine.

Elin Lindström, a winsome, multilingual, quick-witted straw-blond and blue-eyed Swedish lass whose closest friends called her *Doll*. Over the years, more than one male friend, including one U.S. president and a U.S. vice president, teasingly called her *Sweetnips*! "And all the time I thought they were saying *Sweetlips*," she once told Ramsay with a lilting Swedish accent and refreshingly easy blush.

Sometimes Elin laughingly called Ramsay by the odd nickname bestowed upon him by comedian Bob Hope during the summer of 1957. Back then Ramsay worked part-time as a gofer for Mr. Hope's writing team, who were happily ensconced in the well-equipped writing studio set just beyond the swimming pool behind Mr. Hope's big house on Moorpark in L.A.'s Toluca Lake district.

Ramsay smiles as he remembers the particular one-liner he wrote that spawned his nickname, Fingers. Fingers? Well, at least Elin liked it. And wasn't it the name Fingers Ramsay that was painted on a brand-new white Pontiac 6000 sedan used by Ramsay and his high-school buddy, Whizzer Wise, to drive 8,300 miles in less than eight days on a mini spare tire in Brock Yates' 1986 *One Lap of America* motoring event?

Tearfully, and with some trepidation, Ramsay recalls that his best days ever had been spent with his one true love, Marie-Ann. She has been his loving, buttoned-up and smart-as-a-whip spouse for some umpteen years. Now, quite understandably, they were separated.

For the sake of her own sanity, Marie-Ann figured it was time to pull the plug on their marriage. It was probably an accumulation of little things, highlighted by Ramsay's obsession with saving a lifetime accumulation of papers and other crap. He simply found it impossible to ever throw away anything!

Thus, boxes upon boxes were piled high in a barn, a chicken coop, a rental storage unit, plus the garage and basement of their home. It was more than a highly organized and rational *neat freak* like Marie-Ann could stand!

And, of course, Ramsay often thinks about the gentleness and wisdom of his mother, whom he sometimes adoringly referred to as M.C., short for Michigan Catherine.

"May the Lord forever rest with her beautiful soul," murmured one of her elderly blue-haired sisters during the memorial service following Catherine Ramsay's cremation. That sweet sentiment probably would have made Catherine's own secular soul cringe!

Like her only son, she had little tolerance and no patience whatsoever for the bigoted religious and evangelical extremists who now, and seemingly throughout history, have been responsible for so many of the world's problems and conflicts. And one wonders what she'd think about one of her nephews, Donald Conklin, who as an adult married into the Church of Jesus Christ of Latter-Day Saints and spent the rest of his life poking into the lives and private matters of extended family members.

Donald evidently decided he could improve his own standing in the Mormon Church by trying to "rescue Catherine Ramsay's soul for all eternity" by publishing everything about her on the Internet and in his books. It's guys like Don Conklin— programmed by their church to butt into other people's business— who succeed in giving ultra-conservative religions a bad name!

———

The Huron County Jail's most improbable guest of 1996, Alec Ramsay, constantly ponders his father's messy suicide in the laundry room at the family farm house back in 1989, followed just two years later when his mother took her last gasps of breath while Ramsay gently stroked her face as she lay on her deathbed in the main floor bedroom at home.

Ramsay's mind replays over and over the circumstances sur- rounding both deaths and, of course, the subsequent loss of the family farm that had been such an important touch mark in the lives of many generations of the Ramsay and Richmond families.

———

For many years Ramsay had occasionally shared with certain close friends his particularly noxious and disparaging views about lawyers in general and, in particular, the probate judges across Michigan who so frequently pose as objective members of the state's court system while actively seeking to sell their influence and power to the highest bidder.

Should he somehow get untangled from his current legal

predicament, Ramsay seems genuinely engaged with the idea of creating yet another problem for himself by going *lawyer-hunting* with his antique .32-caliber Colt automatic pistol. It's the same weapon his dad used to shoot rattlers in Yellowstone Park during his Ford Model A road trip—from Michigan to Wyoming and back—with a buddy in the mid-1920s. Wow, what an adventure that must have been!

According to Ramsay's late father, it was on that trip that they happened upon John D. Rockefeller, Jr. and his driver standing along the roadside next to their huge black automobile. Ramsay's father and his buddy either repaired or replaced the offending flat tire, enabling Mr. Rockefeller to continue on to his nearby lodge. It's unrecorded as to how deeply disappointed were the two young men at not being invited by Mr. Rockefeller to at least share a hot supper that evening, one undoubtedly prepared by a real chef and served on real china with genuine silverware set on a massive oaken table.

———

Recalibrating his mental gears, Ramsay wonders about the merit of this idea: Why not organize and promote a national day across America dedicated to the proposition of *"Help Free America! Kill A Lawyer Today. And Another One Tomorrow!"*

Ramsay's nasty passion evidently extends to law school students, too. His single semester at the Detroit College of Law somehow must have soured him for a lifetime regarding the law, lawyers and judges. Ramsay wonders how many folks in America can be persuaded to contribute funds and energy to help promote his oddball mission.

———

Suddenly, Alec Ramsay has another mind fart! It occurs to him that, "Sure, there's a better, more practical and doable idea that ought to be added to my list of ultimate pipe dreams!"

He continues, mumbling out loud, "Yeah, that's it . . . *that's* precisely what I need to do. Why not try writing a book while I marinate in this dank, urine-tinged jail cell in the depths of Bad Axe, right in the middle of Michigan's Thumb? *Well sure, why not!*"

Ramsay clearly is smitten with his newest "big idea." But is it for real, or just another of his jailhouse fantasies? Indeed, it might be a way to keep his mind focused, instead of risking that it'll continue turning into mush. Ramsay certainly doesn't need to check his Franklin Planner to know he shouldn't plan on going anywhere, at least not anytime soon. Except to pee and poop in his cell's smelly, coverless toilet.

The toilet reminds Ramsay of the *squats* he's seen, and even used from time to time, in the countryside surrounding cities like Marrakech, Jakarta, Tokyo, Taipei and Seoul. How ironic it now is for him to be stuck in this dim and dingy hellhole, located smack in the middle of possibly the whitest county in all of Middle America.

It strikes Ramsay that perhaps his book can provide an outlet to spew some of the venom that has accumulated with regard to his angry, long simmering estrangement with his only sibling, Wilma. She is, last he'd heard, still the exceedingly pretty snow-haired sister—three years younger than he—who seems married forever to the state of Idaho, homebase for all things *potato* and also headquarters for America's right-wing paramilitary mentality. To Ramsay's way of thinking, Idaho must be one of those places where the words "crazy" and "cult" were coined!

After deep-sixing her life in Michigan sometime in the mid-1960s—during the time Ramsay was living in Manhattan—Wilma swore never to return to her home state. And, although he may quietly wish to see her again, Ramsay's brain cannot jettison the hope she'll remain true to her word. Although invited several times over the years, Wilma and her family have never made the effort to visit her brother and Marie-Ann in their Michigan home. Too bad, so sad!

———

Ramsay again starts mumbling to himself, and ticks off a few of his local heroes. Topping the list is General Motors' highly-creative Swedish-born worldwide purchasing chief, Bo Andersson. Tough as nails, Andersson assumed the mantel of his mentor, Ignacio Lopez, as the automotive industry's number 1 supplier nemesis. Ramsay first came to know Andersson through the Swedish-American Chamber of Commerce. And he appreciated opportunities to spend quality time with "the man" at the Opel plant in Russelsheim, Germany, where Andersson was based as vice president of purchasing for GM of Europe.

Other heroes include retired automotive industry guru Robert Stempel; Jack Kevorkian, the doctor-assisted suicide advocate; and Hubert Humphrey, the former U.S. vice president under U.S. President Lyndon Johnson. Completing the list are three favorite writers: *Detroit Free Press* sportswriter and columnist Mitch Albom, and two extraordinarily talented former Detroit ad agency copywriters, Larry Kasdan and Dutch Leonard. Oh, and two more former advertising copywriters: Fred Doner and Pete DeLorenzo.

———

Inexplicably, the prisoner's muddled mind darts back to a missed opportunity, many years earlier, to nail Marie-Ann's cousin from Stockholm, a Swedish actress and James Bond *flicka* who for a few years had shacked up in the Hollywood Hills with a rock-and-roller named Rod Stewart. The tabloids report that Britt pines for her salad days of the '60s and '70s when she seemingly welcomed all *comers* by wearing a toothy grin on her pretty mug and a smiley face on her clitoris.

———

Suddenly Ramsay leaps up from his cot and turns toward the hallway security camera that monitors his third-floor cell around the clock. In surprisingly precise and measured tones, he begins to address the camera with his twisted interpretation of the relationship between U.S. President George Washington's 1783 farewell speech to his officers at Fraunces Tavern on Pearl Street— in what now is Manhattan's financial district—and the self-fulfilling predicaments that continue to plague countries and dictators throughout the Middle East.

———

"Hey, I really do have a lot to write for . . . I mean *a lot to live for*," the prisoner mutters to himself with a half-crooked smile. "Guess I'll postpone my suicide-by-hanging. The "Big S" will just have to wait!"

The pain in his head has already begun to subside as his fingers roll a blank sheet of white twenty-four-pound 8-1/2 x 11-inch paper into the old typewriter.

Clackety-clack, clackety-clack can be faintly heard in the adjacent cells long after the "house lights" have gone off. With luck, other guests of the county who are ensconced near Ramsay's cell won't piss and moan too loudly during the coming nights and days.

◄ Chapter 2 ►

A Curbside Assassination Shocks Passersby Outside Stockholm's Fabled Grand Hotel

THURSDAY, FEBRUARY 1, 1968

It's almost noon and the sitting U.S. vice president is in Stockholm—Sweden's beautiful and unique island-bound capital city—for a three-day conference of world diplomats. The announced purpose of the meetings is yet another attempt to peacefully and permanently resolve the ongoing Middle East conflict plaguing the Palestinians and the Israelis.

Larry Gartner, chief aide to the vice president, moves toward the huge oval conference table and slips his boss an Associated Press release he just ripped off of the Grand Hotel's teletype machine. It's headlined: *"Former V.P. Richard Nixon officially declares his candidacy for the Republican presidential nomination."* The vice president quietly smiles and then winks at Gartner as if to say, "So, is anybody really surprised?"

As the vice president pushes his chair back from the table, Gartner points out the headline on another European-spec A-sized sheet of paper: *"South Vietnamese Pres. Nguyen Van Thieu declares a nationwide state of martial law as savage fighting continues throughout South Vietnam . . . Viet Cong launch major attacks in the Mekong Delta."*

Barely hiding amusement at his cleverness, Gartner whispers, "I'm sure glad we're in Sweden, where *shooting* only means Ingmar Bergman is filming another movie."

————

Several of the conferees who are particularly close friends stroll out of The Grand Hotel to take lunch together aboard Kurt-Visby Rädisson's 232-foot ocean-going yacht, which is moored just across Strömkajen Drive from the hotel's front entrance. Rädisson is a wealthy middle-aged Swedish-American hotel and service industry magnate from Minneapolis, Minnesota.

Today's luncheon group includes the vice president, who is from Minnesota, and his longtime friend and mentor, Sweden's ultra-liberal Premier Tage Erlander. Another friend is Lars Lindström, a leading Swedish journalist and co-founder of the Stockholm-based International Peace Research Institute, main sponsor of the conference.

As the group of six waits on the sidewalk for the late morning traffic to clear, two gunshots ring out. Heads turn to see which of the passing cars had backfired.

Lars Lindström collapses onto the sidewalk, mortally wounded Pandemonium erupts as folks rush toward Lindström's motion-less body.

A powerful-sounding motorbike pulls around the waiting line of vehicles and makes a sharp right toward Strandvägen and the water alongside the Strand Hotel.

Amidst the confusion, it's unclear as to who was actually the motorbike rider-terrorist's real target. Was it really the mild-mannered Lars Lindström, Sweden's celebrated and highly popular Angel of Peace? Or could it be that the pistol shots actually were intended for Sweden's premier? Or perhaps even the American vice president? Or maybe for the young up-and-coming anti-Vietnam War firebrand named Olof Palme, whom Premier Erlander was carefully grooming for a larger role in Swedish politics?

Plenty of other potential targets were within range, including numerous European, Arab and Israeli diplomats who were also in Stockholm for the peace conference. But the fact remained, it was Lars Lindström who lay dead in the street.

As Sweden's secret police begins the process of locking down Stockholm's perimeter, a telephone call to the Central Police Station alerts authorities that a motorbiker fitting the assassin's description has crashed into a high curb in Stockholm's industrial southside district of Nacka.

Police rush to the scene and find a blue-steel 9-mm pistol glistening in the snow-covered grass near the motorbiker's motionless *and* faceless body. His protective helmet—which Swedish law requires all bikers to wear—is nowhere in sight!

◀ Chapter 3 ▶

*Elin Lindström Receives Horrific News at
Her 220 East 60th Apartment in Manhattan*

THURSDAY, FEBRUARY 1, 1968

It's nearly dawn in Manhattan on Thursday, February 1, 1968. The weather is crisp. Not surprisingly, however, there's no snow on the ground because in the big city, winter temperatures are always a few degrees higher than in the suburbs and the countryside beyond.

Elin Lindström, a portrait photographer with a preference for working with black-and-white film, is dog-tired after working all night. She'd taken only three quick breaks—twice when she had to pee and once when she quaffed a bottle of Coke to rinse down a cold day-old Reuben sandwich. It wasn't exactly the luxurious experience she had anticipated when she accepted the assignment at the palatial home of Mrs. Henry Phipps on Long Island's North Shore.

Elin guides her glistening red 1968 Camaro convertible down the western slope of the Queensboro Bridge and bends slightly right onto East 60th Street, which goes one-way west across Manhattan. Just past Serendipity III on the right and All Saints' Episcopal Church on the left—between 2nd and 3rd Avenues—she turns hard to the left and coasts down the ramp into the garage beneath her apartment building at 220 East 60th.

A signature-blonde, blue-eyed Swede, Elin is a Georgetown-educated, street-smart twenty-eight-year-old woman who is multilingual, speaking fluent Swedish, English, French, Arabic, and Hebrew, plus a smattering of other languages Europeans typically pick up along the way.

In the darker recesses of her mind, Elin harbors a belief that someday she will earn big money in the dangerous and under-publicized netherworld of arms smuggling and third-world finance. Elin has learned important lessons after a few years living with her folks and half-brother in the Middle East. She has paid particular attention to the ins-and-outs of Islam's super-secret banking system. But she realizes, at least for now, *that* surprising career choice must remain on-hold so as not to risk embarrassing her papa and his newspaper back home in Stockholm.

After parking in her reserved spot, Elin opens the trunk. She unloads several pieces of bulky photo equipment and schleps it toward the elevator. After punching "4" she says to herself, "Jeez, a person could make some serious money if they figured out a way to attach wheels to a suitcase. Anything would be better than hauling all this shit on my back. I'm not a pack mule!"

Enough already of this feeling sorry for me, she thinks. The elevator door quietly slides open and Elin wrestles her stuff into the hallway and then drags it toward her apartment at the end of the hall.

As Elin fishes in her purse for the key to apartment 4-C, she hears the muffled sound of her telephone ringing. Scrambling inside, she leaves all of her expensive equipment sprawled on the hallway floor and the apartment door wide open, wondering *Who the devil has balls enough to ring me this early in the morning? Chrissakes, it's not even dawn!*

Snatching up the receiver, Elin switches into her best New Yawk accent and says, "Whom may I ask is calling, and what is it you want at this ungodly hour?"

The voice on the other end surprises her. "Elin, this is Anders

Wallenberg in Washington. I know it's pretty early in the morning for a Swede to be calling anybody. But you'll please need to forgive me."

Holy Smoke, she exclaims to herself, *Why is Sweden's Ambassador to the United States calling me?*

She finds out soon enough, for Ambassador Wallenberg says he's calling to convey terrible news about her father.

"Dearest Elin, it's my unfortunate duty to tell you that your father has been shot and killed in Stockholm." He refrains from telling her too many details, mainly because he doesn't yet know the circumstances surrounding the tragic event.

The charming and patrician ambassador, a favorite at Lyndon Johnson's White House, is particularly careful to remain warm and gracious in expressing his personal condolences, especially since they involve his old friend Lars Lindström, whom Wallenberg and his wife have known since Elin was a youngster.

He tells Elin that he already has taken the liberty of making arrangements for her to be flown to Sweden this very afternoon on his Swedish government-owned SAAB TransContinental.

The ambassador also notes that many of the diplomats already in Stockholm for her papa's peace conference, including America's Vice President Humphrey, plan to remain in Stockholm so they can attend the state funeral that is hastily being planned for Saturday, two days hence.

"Is that all right with you, Elin?" the ambassador gently inquires. Both he and she know that any response from her except "yes" is unacceptable!

Bone-tired after working all night on Long Island, Elin realizes her thinking probably is a little fuzzy. While she won't admit it, Elin is relieved to know that others will be responsible for planning and carrying out the myriad details relating to her father's funeral.

Still trying to focus her mind, Elin thanks the ambassador for his phone call and for considering her best interests.

As she hangs up the receiver, Elin realizes that she's still trying to get over her mother's untimely demise a year earlier. It's going to be an especially difficult time with no mother and, now, no father. The only family member left is her half-brother, George Grant, from whom she has been estranged for many years. Elin predicts that George's main concern will be, "Who's gonna get the antique grand piano?" It's a huge instrument that has sat forever, unplayed and probably untuned, in the main parlor of their parents' home.

◀ Chapter 4 ▶

Awaiting a Silvery Bird in Stockholm's Archipelago

THURSDAY, FEBRUARY 1, 1968

Three rather unpleasant-looking men—shabbily-dressed, dingy, swarthy and grim-faced—are squeezed uncomfortably into a beaten-up cream-colored Volvo Amazon 121 coupé. The car sits semi-hidden beneath a stand of mature spruce trees alongside the crude landing strip carved from a farmer's field northeast of Stockholm. The scene is freshly dusted by a light snowfall.

The two men in the front seat are complaining about something. Their restlessness and concern is obvious.

Evidently some of their concern is caused by a delay in the arrival of a silvery Beech Bonanza. It's already a half hour behind the tight timetable dictated by team members back in Syria. In the coupé's tight backseat is a young man, Tariq Al-Wahid, squeezed in among dirty duffel bags.

Holding onto a heavy, primitive mobile handset, the man in the front passenger seat, who is called Mohammad, receives crackling confirmation that the black-leathered biker—whom they had killed earlier in the day and planted on the street in Nacka—had been found by the police.

A few minutes later, a small V-tailed aluminum-skinned plane descends through the cloud bank, circles the field in a wide sweeping turn and tips its wing just before landing.

Even before the small plane has stopped rolling, Mohammad

and Tariq jump out of the Volvo with the crude radio-telephone and two medium-sized khaki duffel bags and a well-worn and faded cotton laundry bag that first saw life at Teddy's Laundry just off of Harvard Square back in Cambridge, Massachusetts. The black block letters spelling the word "Teddy's," although now faded to grey, are still visible.

Mohammad and Tariq scramble onto the Beech Bonanza's front wing and squeeze into the tiny cabin with their bags, while the pilot checks his gauges and prepares to relight the engine.

There are no goodbyes as the plane bounces along the crude jerry-built strip. The engine roars even louder as the plane reaches the groundspeed needed to catch enough air under the wings to lift quickly off of the ground.

The clunky radio-telephone in Mohammad's hand awakens again with a loud crackle. Less than ten minutes have elapsed into the flight across the Baltic toward a rendezvous point on a grassy strip tucked behind a large commercial produce farm in northern Poland. The two passengers will then transfer to a somewhat larger Russian-built plane for the final leg of their journey to Damascus.

Mohammad reaches forward toward the pilot to borrow an extra headset he sees hanging in the cockpit. He plugs it into his radio-telephone so he can hear above the engine's noise.

The terse message he receives is deeply disturbing. Old man Mohammad's back stiffens and his facial muscles draw tight, making him look even more sinister.

Speaking in Arabic, Mohammad says cryptically, "I agree that the boy's mistake is unfortunate. No, no, it's unforgivable! And by the grace of Allah we shall be able to deal pragmatically with this matter tomorrow in the desert." Mohammad dismisses his caller by saying, "We'll talk later."

As Mohammad hands the headset back to the pilot, he turns and glances at Tariq Al-Wahid in the backseat. If looks could kill, then young Al-Wahid would already be dead. Fortunately for the young man, at least for now, he's fast asleep and hasn't a single clue as to what his future holds.

The odds are it won't be pretty.

◄ Chapter 5 ►

Alec Ramsay Comforts a Distraught Elin Lindström

THURSDAY, FEBRUARY 1, 1968

Although it's barely light outside his Manhattan apartment, Alec Ramsay is already up, showered, shaved and breakfasted. It's his usual six-day-a-week routine before dashing off to his office at J. Walter Thompson Company, the multinational advertising agency at 420 Lexington Avenue that looms above the cavernous Grand Central Station.

Ramsay has choices on how to reach his office. On clear days, he can fast-walk the almost two miles from 220 East 60th to East 44th Street in about a half hour. Or he can walk west past Bloomingdales and catch the southbound subway at 60th and Lex. He knows that the worst alternative is trying to catch a cab, especially anytime during Manhattan's long rush-hour.

This morning, Ramsay's first order of business at the office will be to telephone his dad in Michigan and wish him Happy Birthday. "Yep, Pop turns sixty-four today!" Ramsay will later tell his secretary.

Suddenly there's a loud, frantic knocking on Ramsay's apartment door. Without even taking the precaution of glancing through the security peephole, Ramsay pulls open the door and is startled to see a tired and disheveled Elin Lindström.

It's obvious to Ramsay that his attractive blonde Swedish friend and neighbor at 220 East 60th, whom he sometimes calls *Doll*, has been crying and is in distress.

With uncharacteristic emotion and directness, Elin blurts out, "Alec, I'm all alone. I'm scared and I don't know what to do."

He motions her to hurry inside his place so that other residents along the corridor don't become alarmed by her unexplained histrionics outside his apartment door. It's already too late, because Ramsay sees two heads craning from different doorways down the hallway. But he also understands that these women probably are bored to death, with nothing but time on their hands, and are simply exercising the insatiable curiosity that marks so many Manhattan apartment dwellers.

"For God's sake, Doll, have you been in an accident? Were you mugged? What the hell's happened to you?

Elin is having a hard time trying to explain what has happened to her.

Ramsay is almost shouting as he tells her, "For God's sake, please calm down. Common, kiddo, take it easy. Now, let's start again, and take it s-l-o-w-l-y." He hands her a cup of freshly-brewed El Pico, saying, "Of course it isn't Swedish coffee, but this stuff's almost as strong."

"There's no time now," she protests, "because I have to pack for my flight to Sweden. I'm leaving in just a few hours."

Ramsay looks confused as he snaps, "Okay. Give me the short version!" He listens attentively as Elin tries to explain what has happened.

They warmly embrace. He tenderly kisses her hair, and murmurs, "Be vigilant, my little Ragtop Doll. Call me at the office if you need anything. I mean *anything at all!*" He so wants to tell her, "I love you, dear Elin." But it doesn't seem the right time.

As soon as Elin leaves and closes his apartment door, Ramsay telephones JWT's creative heavyweight, Harry Treleavan, his chief advertising and political mentor at the agency. He knows that Treleavan probably has been at work in his tenth floor office since before six-thirty.

Yes, indeed; Harry admits he's gulping his third cup of Thermos coffee and sucking on his fourth cigarette. And it's not yet half past seven.

The first words spewing from Treleavan's mouth are, "Son-of-a-bitch, Alec . . . they missed the fucking target!"

Ramsay screws up his face, perplexed and confused. "Look, Harry, I'm not sure what's going on. I don't know what you're talking about. All I know is that Elin Lindström was just here and told me that something horrible happened to her dad in Sweden this morning."

Treleavan seems about to come unglued. "What are you saying, Alec? Does she know? It's impossible. There's no fucking way she could know!"

Ramsay is slow to answer. Then he responds slowly, very deliberately, "Harry, I didn't say Elin knows anything. And for damn sure, I don't have a clue as to what the hell you're talking about. All Elin said to me is that the Swedish Ambassador phoned her real early from Washington. He said somebody on a bike shot her dad dead this morning. In Stockholm. Killed him right on the sidewalk!"

◀ Chapter 6 ▶

*The U.S. Vice President Sends Flowers and a
Note to His Young Lady Friend*

Thursday, February 1, 1968

A buzzer sounds in Elin's apartment, startling her as she's folding and packing clothes laid out on the bed.

She presses the call button and finds it's only Spagna, the doorman downstairs, calling to announce that he has an important package for her. She gently tries to put him off.

But Spagna won't be denied. He insists that he really needs to deliver the package right away . . . before the morning traffic gets really busy. Elin relents and says, "Okay, come on up. But I don't have time to chat."

Spagna's rough-hewn countenance and permanent, slightly off-center smile does little to instill confidence in strangers. Elin and Alec Ramsay have never agreed as to whether or not Spagna is queer. Alec says, "Absolutely he is, but there's nothing wrong with that." But Elin's not so sure as she muses, *But how can Alec be so rock-solid confident . . . unless? No, no, no, from our bedding down together I know differently!*

Even though Elin likes and generally trusts Spagna, she is always slightly suspicious. On this morning, her internal warning antenna goes way up—even higher than usual. Told by her papa to always be suspicious of people she doesn't know well, and most particularly strangers bearing unsolicited gifts and favors. Elin is puzzled, curious and more than a little concerned about who is sending her something at such an early hour today. Especially today!

Moments later, Spagna knocks on her apartment door. Elin peeks through the hole, then unchains her door and opens it.

Ever so sweetly, she says, "Mr. Spagna, please be a dear and open the package for me." She discreetly takes a few steps back into her apartment, closes the door part way and catches herself thinking, *Well, at least the paper's pretty . . . and I don't hear any ticking sound!*

Elin listens as Spagna unwraps the package in the hallway. In a moment he pushes the door open and hands her a beautiful flower arrangement. Elin feels a little foolish having made such a fuss over some flowers.

Tucked between the blossoms is a small envelope, which Elin starts to open at the same time she's wrestling to find some tip money. She hands Spagna his usual one dollar bill, and he predictably responds, "Oh, my goodness. Why, thank you, Miss Lindström."

Elin rather enjoys hearing Spagna mispronounce her name. "And thanks for coming up, Mr. Spagna. Please have a wonderful day." The door closes quietly.

Elin's eyes moisten as she carefully opens the envelope and looks at the card inside. There are so many words that the florist must have had trouble transcribing them all on the small card.

She reads quietly to herself: "To one so young, vibrant, intelligent and beautiful, who has now lost her last precious family member. Please be reassured that you are much loved and protected by a gossamer of loving friends. And, my dearest Sweetnips, macabre as it may seem at this moment, I've not forgotten about the few drops of blood I owe you for your outrageously tasteless FLUXUS art project. I shall wait for you in Stockholm. Fondly. Horatio."

Elin smiles and mumbles to herself, "My God, only my Horatio could find a Manhattan florist open this early on a Thursday morning." She really wanted to believe that, even though she knew it must have been Larry Gartner who, however reluctantly, handled the ordering details for his boss.

Opening her bedroom dresser's top right drawer, Elin gently sets the note and envelope atop a stack of others. Some of the envelopes are addressed to "Elin"; others are inscribed to "Ragtop Doll." And two or three simply say "Sweetnips." All are signed by "Horatio," Elin's name for the vice president of the United States.

One rose-colored envelope rivets her attention. She carefully opens it for the umpteenth time and reads again the free verse that Horatio scribbled on vice presidential letterhead and sent to her following last year's trip to Los Angeles. Horatio entitled his love poem, "Recollections of a Santa Monica Mountaineer." The paper, now slightly torn, contains these words:

> Searchlights reach toward the soft, misty clouds.
> The distant drone of an airplane, circling lazily overhead,
>   gently plays with our senses.
> On the far edge of the valley, a powerful beacon calls the
>   airplane home.
>
> Like a carnival of fireflies, headlights twinkle their tortuous
>   way up the mountainside.
> Bright lights in the valley far below, which tonight are gay
>   lights, stretch almost to the boundaries of imagination.
> And they give virility to the night.
>
> Up here, there was only quiet darkness—until you came.
> When that happened, my darkness gave way to a better Dawn.
> Now the light and glow that's me beams brighter than any
>   searchlight blessing clouds or setting an airplane's course.

More luminescent than headlights guiding the way,
More splendid than the beams that every night make your
valley so special.
It makes me love you, Elin, with all that I might.

The score of cities spread-out below us are woven together
by light, just as we are united with the warmth of life.
The same friendly breeze that hums through the trees plays
a melody with your hair and makes me forget my world.
You whisper softly, while you breathe and pulsate more deeply.

In this magical place overlooking your valley—your world—
it's always quiet and peaceful.
Listen to the soft murmur of the valley, the distant yelp of
a dog, and remember the confident, yet flickering, lights
confirm we're not in heaven.
It's ecstasy, and it's all beautiful and good.

Here with you, dearest Elin, parked with top down on
Mulholland Drive . . . high above San Fernando Valley.

Tears well in Elin's eyes as she slips the colored envelope back
into her dresser's drawer.

◄ C h a p t e r 7 ►

Democratic Power Brokers Gather at
Andrew Gallagher Ryan's 16th Street Home in D.C.

THURSDAY, FEBRUARY 1, 1968

Long time Democratic Party operative and founding partner at Washington's venerable Ryan, Bader & Potts on DeSales Street, attorney Andrew Gallagher Ryan, Sr., enjoys a hectic, productive and privileged existence.

Mr. and Mrs. Ryan's fifth floor cooperative apartment on 16th Street overlooks the Washington Hilton, directly across the street. Kitty-corner to the left is the Soviet Embassy. The embassy is a fortress-like building that's permanently festooned with communications antennae of every imaginable size, description and power capacity. The double iron gates guarding the heavy carved oak front door seldom swing open, and then only for invited guests.

Improbably, the hip-happeningest place in Washington, D.C., is the Jockey Club, which is located on the other side of the Ryans' master bedroom wall. Some nights, especially on weekends, the throbbing beat of the loud music makes sleeping difficult which is why the Ryans use heavy-duty his-and-her earplugs to help assure a sound sleep!

Looking to the right from his living room bay window, Ryan can see the White House four short blocks to the south, across from Lafayette Park. The eminent attorney quietly covets the fact that 1600 Pennsylvania Avenue is home to one of Ryan's longest-standing private clients, U.S. President Lyndon Baines Johnson.

It's right here, in the Ryan family's large living room, that significant quantities of America's legislative business during the late 1950s and throughout the 1960s have been initiated, discussed and negotiated. In this very room, under the hand-carved coved ceiling, it's neither unusual nor incongruous to find the Senate Majority Leader, Vietnam War dove Mike Mansfield, talking turkey with the likes of a Vietnam War hawk such as former Defense Secretary Robert McNamara.

And that's just for starters. With Andrew Ryan's involvement, blessing and maybe even a little cash, it seems anything and everything can be arranged.

Ryan's comfortable downtown Washington home is like an off-campus private club for favored senior members of Congress, cabinet officers and occasionally even President Johnson himself.

As President Johnson's personal attorney, Ryan effectively controls, via various trust agreements, the president's and Lady Bird's NBC-affiliated broadcast empire back in Texas. Many other local NBC affiliates are clients, too, plus the National Broadcasting Company itself, which occupies the RCA Building in Manhattan's Rockefeller Center.

Which came first, the power or the profits? In Ryan's case, it was the *power*. The reason: He ran Franklin Roosevelt's Federal Power Commission back in the 1930s, a role which enabled Ryan to build a lifetime network of operatives who ultimately would wield immense power and prestige across the interlocking fabric of American government and business.

Early in his career, Ryan chose to operate mainly on the Democratic side of the political ledger. But that never meant he didn't assiduously cultivate and maintain powerful contacts among Republicans in all corners and levels of American life.

———

It's late morning on February 1, and several members of the Democratic Party's 1968 Presidential Election Committee's brain trust have arrived at Ryan's home to discuss a variety of matters. Topping the agenda is former Vice President Richard Nixon's announcement to the press early this morning saying that he is officially declaring his candidacy for the 1968 Republican nomination. But today's announcement won't put to rest the number 2 question being asked around town: "Why did Mr. Nixon wait so long to announce the obvious?" As with most politically-oriented questions, at best the answer will be highly nuanced; at worst, the question will simply be ignored.

But the number 1 question in Washington and around the country continues to be: Given that the U.S. president can't find an honor able way to extricate American troops from Vietnam, will President Johnson have the stomach to seek re-election on November 5th of 1968?

The general consensus among those who hang out in Ryan's living room is that President Johnson will find some kind of excuse not to run this year. Which leaves another big question: Who will be the Democrat's candidate . . . somebody capable of beating Nixon!

Robert Kennedy can become a strong and well-financed candidate, although he's not trusted by many party leaders. George Wallace has the potential to play the role of a spoiler, but he'll never be elected president by moderate Democrats and independents. President Johnson's vice president, Hubert Humphrey, is a favorite among Ryan's friends. He's a no-nonsense, but likeable, liberal who would have to work extra hard to distance himself from Johnson's policies regarding America's incursion into Vietnam.

In reality, the Democratic National Convention in Chicago during August probably will have to decide between Bobby K. and Hubert H. If the decision were left entirely to the anti-war activist crowd, then Kennedy would be a shoo-in to whip Nixon's ass. His brother did it in 1960; now it's Bobby's turn.

As Ryan's assemblage of colleagues continue to compare notes and trade information on a limitless range of topics, they sip coffee and juice while snacking on Delphine Ryan's homemade French delicacies.

The politicos express appreciation as they sit in comfortable leather sofas and overstuffed chairs that surround the huge perfectly polished antique circular cherry pedestal coffee table. The table's only imperfection is a slight scar which resulted years before when nobody noticed until too late that a cigarette had fallen off an ashtray.

On one wall of the living room are two museum-quality Delacroix oils fitted with hand-carved frames. Friends closest to Andy Ryan know that his wife's family is French, and that her maiden name is Delacroix. It figures!

Michigan's senior U.S. Senator, Phil Hart, asks if anybody else around the table had heard that President Johnson is planning to capture headlines tomorrow by asserting that the Communist offensive in South Vietnam is "a complete failure."

Eyes in the room shift toward Ryan, who shrugs and says, "But what can we do? It's simply political suicide for the president, and it will play right into the hands of Bobby Kennedy and his ilk. And it's not going to get any easier next week, when former Alabama Governor George Wallace is expected to publicly announce his own third-party presidential candidacy."

Some in the room already have heard, via phone calls from President Johnson's appointments secretary at the White House and from Humphrey's prickly aide in Stockholm, Larry Gartner, that the vice president intends to remain in Sweden for an extra day so he can attend the funeral of his dear friend, Lars Lindström.

From a Democratic National Committee tap on Harry Treleavan's personal line at JWT in Manhattan, and another one on John Mitchell's law office telephone down on Wall Street, Ryan already knows that Richard Nixon won't be going to Stockholm. Such a trip was probably a non-starter anyway inasmuch as Nixon had never met Lindström, and such a mission would be viewed by *The New York Times'* Tom Wicker and others in the so-called establishment press as blatant political opportunism.

For just an instant, Ryan reflects back on how Harry Treleavan had been asked in early 1966 by Nagib Halaby, president and CEO at one of JWT's long time clients, Pan American World Airways, to take a leave of absence to work on a long-shot Republican congressional campaign in Lyndon Johnson's home congressional district in Texas.

Treleavan finally agreed to help, but only on weekends. So, for a few months during 1966, he would leave JWT at noon on Fridays and arrive back in his office before noon on Mondays, after spending his weekend in Texas plotting political strategy and crafting communication messages for George Herbert Walker Bush.

Thanks mainly to Treleavan's efforts, and significant amounts of money raised by a handful of hardcore Texas Republicans like businessman and yachtsman Robert Mosbacher, the practically unknown candidate for the U.S. Congress ultimately was elected as the first-ever Republican U.S. Representative in Johnson's heretofore overwhelmingly Democratic stronghold.

Winners like winners! And Mosbacher—who was accustomed to winning, whether he was competing in business, politics or in the America's Cup, which was won in 1963 by his twelve-meter yacht *Weatherly*—really liked Treleavan! Who else could have crafted George H. W. Bush's first-ever political victory? And thanks in large measure to Bob Mosbacher, Harry Treleavan was acclaimed as a new breed of political strategist and marketing genius. And best of all, Harry was a Republican.

Ryan still shivers at his recollection of President Johnson's day-long towering rage in early November 1966, triggered when the president awoke the morning after that Texas election and asked for the results. From the moment he heard about Bush's victory, nothing would ever again be considered to be a sure thing for Lyndon Baines Johnson.

Many of Johnson's closest advisors agreed that—thanks in large measure to Harry Treleavan's 1966 heroics in Texas—the fun and euphoria of politics and the governing of America had been exchanged for wearisome drudgery.

A few fair-weather Democratic loyalists in the Johnson White House were already beginning to spend uncommon amounts of time outside their offices having lunch and dinner with friends and lobbyists who might be useful in helping to line up fresh careers. Many ultimately became Washington lobbyists and representatives serving big-money interests both in America and around the world.

There could be no doubt that the plug had been pulled from the Johnson presidency, and the rats were scurrying down the ropes and gangplanks!

◄ Chapter 8 ►

A Scar-Faced, Greasy-Haired Stranger
Lurks on the Sidewalk Across from Elin's Apartment

THURSDAY, FEBRUARY 1, 1968

"Good afternoon, Miss Lindström. Hope you had a nice lunch. I have your cab waiting." The greeting was Spagna's stilted attempt to make stimulating conversation.

At least I guess he's trying, Elin thinks to herself.

It's early afternoon on Thursday, February 1, and Spagna holds wide open the apartment building's heavy, extra wide glass front door. Elin doesn't wait for the doorman to grab her medium-sized blue Samsonite bag with the wide yellow and blue band around it. Instead, she effortlessly carries the bag down the two wide steps, steps briskly across the sidewalk and tosses her bag onto the back seat of the Yellow cab Spagna had hailed just moments after Elin buzzed him from upstairs.

She jumps in next to her bag and barks instructions to the driver, "North entrance of the Pan Am Building, across from 45 Park. And go quickly, please." The cabbie was impressed by Elin's physical strength and her ability to give specific directions. He thinks, *This chick's no sucker!*

As the taxi pulls away from the curb, neither Elin nor Spagna notice the sun-glassed dark-haired man across the street who has been watching Elin's departure from the doorway of Serendipity III, the trendy Manhattan restaurant and celebrity hangout.

The almond-skinned man with greasy hair has a deep scar

running from his mid-forehead down across the left eyebrow to his lower jaw. The stranger continues watching the cab until it catches the green light at Third Avenue. Then he turns around slowly and disappears into the restaurant.

Only the Lord knows what the fancy-pants late-luncheon types inside must have thought when they saw this unforgettably disheveled and unattractive person enter their territory. He boldly walked through the swinging kitchen door and out the restaurant's back door into the alley.

◄ **Chapter 9** ►

Lifting Off from Atop Manhattan's Pan Am Building

Thursday, February 1, 1968

At precisely 2:30 p.m. on Thursday, February 1, 1968, Pan Am's Sikorsky helicopter Flight 007 gingerly lifts off the pad atop the Pan Am Building for its ten-minute hop to JFK. Flying so low over the rooftops of Manhattan and Queens is an exhilarating experience; one which Elin might have enjoyed more under less-trying circumstances.

Elin leans forward in her seat and easily squints toward the southwest, trying to see the sixteen-acre World Trade Center site where construction of two identical towers began two years earlier. Much closer to the Pan Am Building are the landmark Empire State and Chrysler buildings. She can also make out the River House apartments on East 54th at the East River, where longtime Lindström family friends, theatrical producer Alexander Ramsey and musical-actress wife, live when they're not in London or at home on their ranch in Brasil, as they call it, considering "Brazil" to be too parochial and over-Americanized.

As Manhattan fades into the distance behind her, Elin is drawn to reflect upon her own mortality, and upon the exceptionally fine life she's enjoyed despite her dear mother's touch of mental disease and eventual premature death from a brain aneurysm.

Now Elin is left all alone to deal with her papa's sad and unexpected demise. Certainly she doesn't expect any support nor much sympathy from her estranged half-brother, George Grant, who operates Grant's Taverna, a popular eating and drinking spot on Stockholm's Strandvägen, not too far from the popular Strand Hotel.

Most of all, Elin regrets not having had a chance to say a proper goodbye to either of her deceased parents. Oh, if only she could have kissed each one again on their foreheads before they died, and thanked them for giving her life!

Although she realizes that the circumstances of her papa's death were beyond her control, Elin already has vowed never to forget nor forgive. She realizes that, sadly, there's probably little she can do to somehow even the score. But, then, who knows what the future may hold! Isn't it supposed to be full of odd twists and turns?

Elin's mind wanders absentmindedly as she ponders the two years she spent working for Pan American World Airways. First she was at the Pan Am office on Washington's K Street, just west of 16th. Then she was invited to New York City, where she worked out of Pan Am's midtown Manhattan headquarters right at the head of Park Avenue North. It was an amazing, stimulating period in her life which had sped by too fast as she worked hard trying so hard to serve two masters, Pan Am and herself.

Until fairly recently, Elin's primary loyalty had been to Pan Am. Nowadays, her main interest is—without any doubt— herself! Elin's single-minded ambition is to be totally independent of others. To her, that means becoming exceedingly wealthy. With her papa now dead in Stockholm, maybe she can start pursuing serious money-making dreams.

Between her assignments as a so-called society portrait photographer, Elin tries hard to mesh her day job with the creation and sale of original FLUXUS art projects. Although Manhattan and

Wiesbaden are ancestral homes for the FLUXUS art movement, Elin's offbeat projects have been slow to catch on with collectors. A notable exception is a forward-looking husband-and-wife team of serious FLUXUS art collectors in Bloomfield Hills, Michigan, Gil and Lila Silverman.

And, of course, Elin is thankful for the opportunity to handle, *sub-rosa*, a variety of G2-type assignments for both the Swedish government and for her highly placed friend in Washington, D.C., a former U.S. senator from Minnesota and now vice president of the United States.

Overall, Elin is quite pleased with herself, knowing she's able to juggle so many varied tasks. Indeed, she has managed to fashion a unique and interesting life.

————

On January 20, 1965, Hubert Humphrey had been sworn in as vice president of the United States. His job was to assist U.S. President Lyndon Baines Johnson, a man who had served without a vice president since unexpectedly assuming the presidency on November 22, 1963, at the airport in Dallas, Texas.

Clearly, Elin Lindström has demonstrated that she knows how to cultivate friends in the highest echelons of government, business and the arts, in America and elsewhere. One of her not-so-secret weapons is her excellent command of several languages. Plus, her beauty, style and grace have proven to be important assets.

————

It was in the spring of 1966 that Elin Lindström first met Lisa Halaby, daughter of Pan Am's President and CEO, Nagib

Halaby. In Elin, the young Lisa had seen almost a spitting-image of what she hoped to become.

When Elin realized that Lisa was highly motivated to learn and speak Arabic because of her family's Lebanese background, it was Elin, already quite fluent in the language, who took her young friend aside and prescribed the foundation of classical Arabic language and culture that would benefit young Lisa for the rest of her life.

About twelve years later, the by then Princeton-educated, highly accomplished and attractive bottle-blonde daughter of Elin's old boss at Pan Am would become engaged to marry Jordan's King Hussein. The future Queen Noor would become King Hussein's fourth wife, and the second Westerner he had married, the first being a British woman.

———

It's almost 2:45 p.m. when the Sikorsky gently sets down, with its usual pinpoint accuracy, onto the tarmac at JFK.

Waiting less than a soccer field's length away from the copter is the Swedish ambassador's thirty-six-passenger SAAB airplane, reconfigured to carry sixteen passengers plus crew. In a short time, the SAAB will depart on its long journey to Sweden, carrying Elin directly to Stockholm and her dear papa's funeral. The sad event already is scheduled for two days later, Saturday, February 3.

For some reason, Elin remembers that the initials SAAB stand for Svenska Aeroplan AB. Her papa once explained how a few key designers at SAAB decided to try their hand at designing and building an automobile that incorporated basic aerodynamic principles.

The aircraft designers were so focused on the overall big-picture design concept that they literally forgot to design taillights for their first prototype. Realizing too late their mistake, the folks at SAAB installed on the prototype two taillights from an early-model Volkswagen Beetle. That first little black Saab coupé is proudly displayed today in the Saab Museum near the Göta Kanal on the west end of Trollhättan, Sweden.

◄ **C h a p t e r   1 0** ►

Richard Nixon's Presidential Campaign
Headquarters in Midtown Manhattan

THURSDAY, FEBRUARY 1, 1968

It's late afternoon on Thursday, February 1, 1968, less than nine hours after Richard Milhous Nixon has announced that he's entering the 1968 U.S. presidential sweepstakes . . ."to win". Nixon's law partner, Big John Mitchell, momentarily ignoring the man seated across the desk, is chomping on the stem of his unlit pipe as he sits behind a gigantic hand-carved oak desk in what is now the Nixon presidential campaign headquarters on upper Park Avenue in midtown Manhattan.

Mitchell jots a note on his pad: "Urgent . . . talk with Walter Annenberg and Peter Clark about using their *Philadelphia Inquirer* and *Detroit News* newspapers to frame editorial policy that local and national media can pick up to help endorse and promote Nixon's candidacy."

Mitchell reaches for his pocket-sized flamethrower and lights the tobacco packed tightly in his pipe. Drawing deeply on the stem, he addresses Harry Treleavan: "Okay, Harry, let's not put lipstick on a pig." As is his wont, Mitchell is talking *at* Treleavan rather than *to* him. "Plain as I can say it, Harry, now that we have an official candidate, your people gotta stop trying to fuck my people."

"For the record, my friend, let's go over this just one more time." Mitchell's voice is brittle and as it rises in volume, his secretary shuts the office door. "You've been invited to be the communications strategist and the advertising brains for this operation. And whether you like it or not—whether you agree or not—the boss has anointed me as his *political* genius. It's okay if you want out now . . . if you don't want to play by my rules! But I really like you, Harry, and the boss and I hope you'll stay. Now understand this doesn't necessarily mean I'm smarter than you. It just means I'm the guy *in charge!* I run the election team. And you and your agency guys are on the team. But it's my team. Do you get it, finally? Any questions, Harry?"

Harry rapidly rolls things over in his mind. *Hmmm, I wonder how Nixon-the-Candidate fits into Mitchell's overall scheme of things? Mitchell's team? It just seems sort of cockeyed!*

Mitchell just won't let up as he raises his voice. "Look, we've talked about this stuff before, but you keep backsliding on me, Harry. You think you're a big deal just because you got George Bush elected to Congress two years ago! Now mark this once and for all: Your main job—in fact, really your only job in 1968— is to build and manage the illusion that Richard Nixon, fifty-four-year-old man of the American people, considers his *communications with the American people* to be both the ultimate privilege and one of the great joys of seeking the U.S. presidency!"

Treleavan, in concert with Frank Shakesphere, Ruth Jones, Al Scott and others on the core communications team, has already concluded that short television commercials—no more than thirty or sixty seconds in length—will become the norm for the Nixon campaign. They'll be used exclusively throughout the Republican Party's 1968 presidential campaign.

———

Meanwhile, over on Madison Avenue—only a few blocks away at the legendary Doyle Dane Bernbach advertising agency—strikingly similar media-strategy conversations are taking place.

In 1964, this traditional Democratic Party ad agency created the classic and emotionally seminal "Little Girl/Daisies/Atomic Bomb Countdown" television spot that effectively torpedoed and sank Republican Barry Goldwater's presidential aspirations and candidacy. And, thanks to Jim Graham's money-saving strategy, that sixty second political commercial—with its extraordinarily powerful graphic and verbal messages—ran only one time on American television! Word-of-mouth did the rest of the damage to Goldwater.

And now in 1968, DDB's political boss man, Joe Napolitan, has also decided to go exclusively with "short format" TV commercial messages. Both Napolitan and Bill Bernbach already have Democratic National Committee board approval no matter whether the anointed Democratic candidate is President Johnson or somebody else.

———

The Republicans' Big John Mitchell and Harry Treleavan will probably never learn about—indeed, they must never know—Elin Lindström's role in causing the Democratic presidential campaign team to re-address and fine-tune its 1968 media strategy.

It's all thanks to some ill-advised and loose pillow talk a week or so earlier between Elin and one of Treleavan's boys from JWT, Alec Ramsay.

———

Overshadowing almost everything else is the fact that it's already February and there's not even one announced Democratic candidate for U.S. President. Granted, it's probably President Johnson's nomination for the taking. But if he decides not to run, then by far the strongest prospect is New York State's junior U.S. Senator Robert F. Kennedy.

Kennedy seems to be making all the right moves. Certainly he is making lots of noise daily in the national and international newspapers. The third-youngest Kennedy brother's media strategy is to release—once each day, without fail—at least one carefully crafted, strongly reasoned and highly-orchestrated press release that methodically attacks President Johnson's positions and credibility on almost every issue, including America's role in what Republicans call the Vietnam War and Democrats refer to as the Vietnam Conflict.

RFK's unrelenting and withering attacks on LBJ's programs are exacting a toll on both the sitting U.S. president and his political advisors, including Vice President Humphrey. Indeed, RFK views Humphrey as the strongest threat to his own nomination at the 1968 Democratic National Convention in Chicago. Humphrey knows, of course, that he's trapped between a rock and a hard place—between President Johnson and Senator Kennedy. At least for now, Humphrey can't appear to be disloyal to Johnson.

RFK seems determined to do everything possible to embarrass President Johnson into renouncing the presidency that was handed to him, for free, five years earlier in Dallas, Texas.

Lyndon Johnson became John Kennedy's vice presidential nominee after Bobby Kennedy's best bud, Missouri's U.S. Senator Stuart Symington, thought *he* had the position locked up. It was only at the last minute that Lyndon Johnson literally went to John F. Kennedy's Chicago hotel room and blackmailed the 1960

Democratic presidential nominee into naming him—already the majority leader of the U.S. Senate—as his party's vice presidential nominee. It was a classic eleventh-hour, heavy-handed political and personal squeeze play. Symington got squat, whereas Johnson moved himself into a position that ultimately enabled him to become the U.S. president!

Precisely what happened is that Johnson point-blank told the first Catholic presidential candidate that he, Johnson, could easily steer the election toward the Republican candidate. Johnson said the choice was JFK's alone. After assessing Johnson's bare-knuckled threat and undeniable political strength, JFK believed he was boxed in and had no choice but to select Johnson as his vice president. It was a decision that JFK, RFK and America would later regret.

Indeed, Robert F. Kennedy never forgave Johnson for apply-ing strong-arm tactics to JFK. But they were not much different than the hardball tactics RFK often used after he became his own brother's attorney general.

Thanks to attorney Andrew Ryan's tentacles, which reached into nearly all facets of Washington, D.C., life, Lyndon Johnson came to know a lot about JFK's extracurricular social activities and various questionable financial matters involving JFK him-self, the Kennedy clan and certain top-echelon mobsters from Boston, Chicago, and Las Vegas. FBI director J. Edgar Hoover also kept Johnson informed regarding JFK's activities.

It's no wonder, then, that Robert Kennedy is so passionate and proactive in his dislike—no, downright hatred—for Lyndon Johnson. It's the main force driving RFK to replace Johnson as the Democratic candidate in 1968.

‹ Chapter 11 ›

A Non-Traditional Funeral Unfolds in Classical Stockholm

SATURDAY, FEBRUARY 3, 1968

By late Friday afternoon on February 2, 1968, arrangements for the next day's funeral were finalized in Stockholm by Swedish government officials, with the general approval of Elin Lindström.

Elin insisted that the funeral service at the historic Riddarholms Cathedral in Old Town start precisely at 11:50 a.m., exactly forty-eight hours after her papa was mysteriously gunned down less than one-thousand meters across the water from where she is now standing near Sweden's Royal Palace.

Elin had three main reasons to justify her burial request.

First and above all, Elin wants to honor her father's wish that upon his death he would be buried quickly as possible, even if the timing wasn't precisely within the limitations of the Muslim and Jewish customs and traditions he so respected and held in high esteem . . . even though he and his family claimed to be secular.

Second, many of her papa's friends from the international community had chosen to remain in Stockholm to continue the same Middle East peace meetings that may have precipitated Lars Lindström's death.

And finally, a quick burial would reduce the window of opportunity for vultures in the world press to converge upon a wintry, dark and shocked Stockholm. Elin was convinced that they would try to unleash the same sort of distasteful and emotionally packed media feeding frenzy that, now more than ever before, seemed to have become a hallmark of terrible events involving high-profile individuals.

John F. Kennedy was perhaps more than a casual acquaintance of Elin's, and she never forgot the unforgivable media coverage that accompanied his death and subsequent funeral, which she watched aghast on television.

The bottom line for Elin is this: While she knows that matters have moved far beyond her control, at the same time she needs to minimize the possibility that some folks—both inside and outside of the media—may begin to craft a mythology around her papa's sudden and tragic demise.

———

Elin quietly reflects upon the tragedy and terror of November 22, 1963. For her, President Kennedy's death was a watershed event.

Vivid memories of JFK fill her head, and tears well in her eyes as she stands alone outside Sweden's Royal Palace in Stockholm's Gamla Stan, or Old Town. Elin treasures the memories of her few visits to the Kennedy White House, where she had swam and partied in the basement pool with staff members and a few outsiders. Occasionally, the president took a break and came down from his office upstairs. It was pretty heady stuff for a Georgetown University grad student from Sweden.

Indeed, it was JFK who befriended Elin by introducing her to his old friend and political ally, Hubert Humphrey, then the senior U.S. senator from Minnesota. That introduction was destined to change Elin's young life in so many ways. And perhaps Humphrey's, too.

————

It was directly across the narrow Riddarsholm canal from where Elin now stands, near the Swedish government offices, that Lars Lindström first practiced and perfected an art form that he soon would take to a higher level: *the art of using the press to influence Sweden's foreign policy.*

Soon after his graduation from the Institute of Journalism in Göteborg, on Sweden's picturesque West Coast, Lindström began to build his credentials as a young reporter. Later he became an editor at the larger of the two newspapers in Eskilstuna. Eskilstuna, best known for its stainless steel manufacturing, is ninety kilometers west of Stockholm on the road to Örebro.

A few years later, soon after Elin's birth, Lindström was offered an extraordinary opportunity—at least for a Swedish print reporter —to become a globe trotting journalist. Thus it was that the Lindström family eventually came to live in Jerusalem and Amman, where they thoroughly enjoyed learning about divergent cultures and the various challenges presented by life in the Middle East.

Lars Lindström's Swedish passport and press credentials were like a magic carpet that enabled him to gain access to people in many global hot spots. Most of Lindström's contemporaries in the working press—from Stockholm to New York to Tokyo— could only fantasize about doing just once what Lindström got to do almost every day. By any measure, life was full and interesting for Lindström and his family, even though it was not so financially enriching. Print journalists don't expect to make lots of money, unless they write a popular book!

————

In her reverie, Elin is momentarily swept away by the fact that some of the pallbearers gathered nearby are dressed in their national costumes, which she thinks looks particularly striking and colorful against the backdrop of Gamla Stan's centuries-old grey stone buildings and Sweden's strong tradition of western culture and modern technology.

Elin thinks it's somewhat ironic that Sweden's main representative at her papa's funeral is Sweden's Prime Minister Tage Erlander, while Erlander's longtime American friend and confidant, Hubert Humphrey, is representing the United States of America and its Vietnam War-plagued President Lyndon Johnson.

Although she has met the Swedish leader once or twice before, thanks to her papa's influence, Elin has on her own initiative become an intimate friend of the American. She's really proud of that accomplishment—her friendship with an American vice president—and the fact she did it by herself in a strange land.

————

During the less-than-five-kilometer funeral procession route from Riddarholmskyrkan to the old Naval Graveyard on Djurgårdsbrön, Elin will notice that the distinctive, graphically strong yellow and blue Swedish national flags are waving at half mast from buildings all along the route and throughout the entire city of Stockholm. With maybe one exception!

For some reason, the Swedish flag hoisted in front of Grant's Taverna, on the north side of Strandvägen three blocks east of the Royal Dramatic Theatre, has not been lowered. At least not yet. The proprietor, George Grant, is Elin's estranged half-brother and Lars Lindström's stepson. Sadly, Elin and George haven't spoken in years.

———

As soon as he has helped hoist the heavy golden-colored oak coffin onto the horse-drawn caisson, Vice President Humphrey spots Elin. Without fanfare, he quietly excuses himself from the swarm of dignitaries awaiting the start of their old friend's final march back to the earth.

In response to the vice president's gracious and softly-uttered greeting, Elin replies "Nonsense, Horatio! Thank you so much for being here for Papa and me. It means so much to *us!*"

Humphrey's face flushes when he realizes that nearby ears are straining to hear his exchange with the grieving only daughter of Lars Lindström. He knows, too, that she's the only person on earth who addresses America's vice president by his middle name!

Elin asks Vice President Humphrey to please ride with her in the first limousine trailing the caisson that is carrying her father. Humphrey gladly accepts, of course, and is delighted to find Prime Minister Erlander already seated inside the heavily armored triple-black stretch Volvo that Gunnar Engellau arranged to have delivered to Stockholm yesterday from Volvo's headquarters in a northwest suburb of Göteborg.

Four muscular, armed and good-looking security staff members from the American Embassy and the Swedish prime minister's security office take up positions next to Elin's car. They'll walk or trot alongside the Volvo during the entire trip to the Naval Graveyard in Djurgården.

◄ Chapter 12 ►

*Giving Lars Lindström Back to the Earth at
Sweden's Historic Naval Graveyard in Djurgården*

SATURDAY, FEBRUARY 3, 1968

It seems fitting that Sweden's historic Naval Graveyard sits
along the edge of the water, and just behind Stockholm's Nordiska
Museet on Djurgårdsvägen. Only a few hundred meters further
along the handsomely curved and tree-lined avenue is Skansen.

Spring and summer—with their continuous and extraordinary
array of plantings and colorful flowers—are the prettiest seasons
at Skansen. Skansen is Sweden's closest equivalent to America's
Colonial Williamsburg in Virginia, and Henry Ford's Greenfield
Village in Dearborn, Michigan.

As the lead car in the long funeral procession draws to a stop
inside the main gate of the Naval Graveyard, a security man catches
up to the lead limousine and opens the passenger-side rear door. Elin,
dressed in a simple black outfit, steps out with a certain practiced
aplomb, grace and elegance. She stands to one side as the U.S. vice
president and the Swedish prime minister exit with far less dexterity.

Even as her eyes grow accustomed to the bright wintry midday
sunlight, Elin can't help but notice the good-looking young man
moving rapidly through the throng toward her. He's wearing a
uniquely shaped lapel pin that the Swedish security team members
seem to recognize.

The fellow approaches Elin, whose glistening white smile—
despite the circumstances—is now competing with the winter

sunshine. Before either utters a word of greeting, the man snaps a photograph of Elin standing between Erlander and Humphrey.

Hans Belfrage is a Stockholm attorney who has known Elin since they were youngsters growing up near Millesgården in the upscale Lidingö Island section of Stockholm. They blow air kisses to each other and then gently hug. Belfrage whispers, "I'm so sorry, my dear."

Elin turns to Vice President Humphrey and introduces him to Belfrage, who is blond, brown-eyed and impeccably dressed. She explains to the American vice president that Belfrage is a high-profile Stockholm attorney who graduated from Stockholm University's Law School, and then practiced law in Sweden for two years before moving to Ann Arbor to do graduate studies at the University of Michigan's Law School.

"In fact," she adds, "it was Hans who introduced me to Alec Ramsay on my first visit to Ann Arbor. Horatio, I think you'll remember Alec. He's the fellow I told you about who was young Andy Ryan's fraternity brother at Michigan. In the DEKE house, I think they called it."

Humphrey's mind seems momentarily in another zone . . . and, as so often happens with politicians, he simply nods in the affirmative.

Elin rattles on, "And it was Alec who, on a lark and without asking Hans' permission, entered him in the 1963 U.S. National Table Tennis Championships at Detroit's Cobo Hall. Hans surprised everyone, except maybe himself, by winning the United States Men's Novice Singles title that year. It was amazing!"

"Good God, my pet, that all seems so long ago," interrupts Belfrage. "You have a marvelous *re-memory*." They laugh.

Vice President Humphrey mumbles something about having played some pretty good table tennis himself early on when he taught at the University of Minnesota and at the toney Macalester College, also in Minnesota. He matter-of-factly says to Belfrage, "Call me next time you're in Washington, and we can play a match or two and have dinner. I think you know how to reach me!" Elin smiles.

By now, the coffin has been off-loaded from the caisson and is being carried slowly to the fresh gravesite that had been dug by hand in yesterday's late afternoon winter semi-darkness. The grave diggers started immediately after Elin had signed off on the site right next to her momma's grave.

Her mother's parents—Elin's *mormor* and *morfar*—also are buried in the Naval Cemetery plot because Elin's grandfather, John Eklund, had been a Swedish naval commander with long and distinguished service as aide-de-camp to Sweden's King Gustav V, who reigned from 1907 to 1950.

Before that, Commander Eklund had been in charge of the four-hundred-year-old monolithic granite fortress on picturesque and storied Marstrand Island, only a short distance by water north of Göteborg on Sweden's rugged West Coast.

Maybe that's why Marstrand, and the granite-encrusted coast northward toward Fiskebäckskil, just across the Gullmarnsfjorden from Lysekil, was always Elin's favorite place growing up—especially during the idyllic sun-bathed months of late June, July and August.

And, of course, Elin loves the fact that her mother was born in the centuries-old stone house just across from the fortress' main entrance. She secretly harbors the idea of maybe one day buying the grand old house and turning it into a health spa where wealthy women from Stockholm, the Middle East and maybe even the United States can come almost year round to luxuriate and spend lots of money.

———

In another unexplainable moment of *strangeness*, possibly attributable to his fatigue, Vice President Humphrey draws Elin aside and whispers something she had heard him say other times in other places, including last year in Paris: "Whether I'm at home in Washington or in Minnesota," he begins, "there's simply nobody around the house who seems interested and in tune with my ideas and aspirations. No one but you, my lovely Elin, seems to share my ambition for accomplishment, recognition and success in public service. After all this time, it's such a shame and it makes me sad."

"Dearest Elin," continues Horatio—it's almost like the vice president is composing another letter to her—"Although we both know it's impossible for ours to be a traditional relationship, I want you to know that you are truly the only person I can trust to share little moments and keep big secrets. And I appreciate that so much more than you can possibly know. Nothing has changed between us, and I'm still willing to risk consequences, if you are."

Elin nods slightly, and discreetly brushes her friend's shoulder with her left hand. A pleasant shiver runs along his penis.

Hesitating for a long moment, Humphrey glances toward his security squad, and then turns back toward Elin. He quietly whispers his proposal that they should share dinner tonight.

"Look," he says softly, "I know it's been another long and lousy day. And, of course, it's entirely up to you." He pauses. "I know it's selfish for me to ask such a thing on the very day we're placing your dear papa to rest."

"No, no . . . *no*," Elin protests, "It's actually such a marvelous idea. Let's do it. We both need to get away from all these people— to simply disappear for a few hours."

A lone trumpeter blows the Swedish equivalent of *Taps* as Lars Lindström's wooden coffin is rendered slowly and lovingly into the ground, hard by the graves of Elin's momma and grandparents, and generations of Sweden's most famous conquering heroes and naval elite. In the distance, a bagpipe drones on.

A twenty-one cannon salute arcs over the hulk of the old Vasa warship, which lies at rest just down the shore. It's on a huge cradle, enclosed within a gigantic plastic tent while constantly being sprayed with a fine mist of specially prepared wood preservatives. The huge 1600s-era wooden ship is being slow-dried in preparation for permanent display after being raised from the coarse bottom of Stockholm's harbor in the early 1960s.

For the first time on this long day, Elin strains to hold back tears as the large group of family friends and dignitaries begins to envelop her.

Standing alone and all but forgotten at the grave hole's edge, peering down at his stepfather's coffin, is George Grant. Elin had decided earlier in the day not to go out of her way to accord him the privilege and favor of being introduced to Sweden's prime minister and the American vice president.

It is Elin's fervent hope that one day she and George can amiably resolve whatever differences they share. After all, each is the only remaining family member the other has. *But,* Elin muses to herself, *does George understand and care as much as I do?*

◄ Chapter 13 ►

His Donkey's Red Ribbon Meets
Tariq's Penis in Syria's Countryside

SATURDAY, FEBRUARY 3, 1968

It's nearing mid-afternoon and a shaggy, forlorn-looking donkey sure footedly carries a bearded old man, dressed in musty, dusty tattered clothing, along the boulder-strewn road toward a fateful meeting. The slope-shouldered rider with a creased and weathered face resembles almost every male his age in Syria. The critter plods along a hard-packed trail leading off the secondary road, usable only during dry weather, connecting Damascus with Khirbet An-Nbash and Zilaf to the southeast.

Even though the country of Jordan is only twenty miles from Zilaf, it's virtually impossible to travel there by animal or vehicle because the region's rugged terrain has made road building cost prohibitive. Moreover, Jordan's King Hussein and Syria's long time military dictator probably agree on only one thing outside of their religion: The less contact there is between their two Islamic fiefdoms, the better.

The weathered traveler and his steed draw up in front of a sturdy-looking one-story mud and stone building. A makeshift affair, made from the abandoned tent of a sheepherder, is draped from the roof to help protect the entrance from the blazing sun and unpredictable torrential rains. Of no less importance is the fact that the solitary sentry can stand virtually undetected in the dark shadows created by large folds in the heavy, almost carpet-like material.

A half dozen donkeys are tied up to nearby scrub bushes. Each animal has a different colored ribbon around its neck. Dismounting, the old man walks over to one of the animals, cuts the wide red ribbon from around its neck and stuffs it inside his outer garment.

————

Once he's inside the weather-beaten building, the old man takes off his long, hooded and dust-caked jalleba, revealing casual western-style garb underneath. It's not exactly Brooks Brothers, but in the Syrian countryside . . . close enough!

Several men are sitting on the floor around a low table in what is apparently the building's main room. With little daylight peeking in from outside, the room is lit mainly by flickering oil lamps. On a side shelf are two large, heavy and expensive Swedish crystal bowls, which are seldom seen outside of the finest homes. Each bowl contains a single large desert scorpion struggling to climb the smooth vertical sides of their respective prisons.

Except for an unsmiling younger man seated at one end of the table, the men scramble to their feet when the old man enters the room. The elders bow slightly in deference, compete to kiss the back of his right hand and greet the visitor by his Arabic name, Mohammad Al-Wahid.

The status of the younger man is not immediately clear. Is he injured, or merely being disrespectful? Or does he remain seated for some other reason?

————

Suddenly, it hits us! We've seen both the older man and the younger man two days earlier, when they were waiting in the old

Volvo Amazon coupé for the Beech Bonanza to land in the field northeast of Stockholm.

On the table in front of the young man are several large heavy clay goblets. Some are empty; a few are still full to the brim with koumis, which is traditional fermented goat's milk. The younger man is actively being encouraged—or cajoled; no, he's actually being forced—to drink *all* of the liquid remaining in the goblets.

When the containers are nearly empty both the *mentor,* a senior elder whose face reveals years of stressful living, and Mohammad Al-Wahid lead the obviously disoriented younger fellow into an adjoining room that is windowless.

The young man is asked to lie face-up on a low wooden platform. His feet and hands are then shackled to each corner.

Mohammad Al-Wahid removes a length of 7-1/2 millimeter-wide red ribbon from his breast pocket and hands it to the *mentor,* who then with some ceremony ties the ribbon tightly around the young man's limp penis. The fellow's face grimaces with a blend of surprise and pain. Unfortunately for the young man, he is not to be a willing nor happy participant in this ultra-conservative religious drama. And he knows it!

His face now frozen with fear, the young man watches silently as the *mentor* turns a large woven basket onto its side. The two large, lethal horned vipers slither onto the dirt floor of the stuffy, thick-walled, windowless room that is lit by a single short wax candle. Inexplicably, the desert scorpions remain in the bowls on the table in the other room.

Moving quickly toward the door, the *mentor* exits into the central room as Mohammad Al-Wahid turns and says matter-of-factly, "Goodbye, my son."

He continues, "In the eyes of Allah and all that is good, sometimes only fractions separate heroes from those unable to become heroes. Perhaps you'll win in another life, dear Tariq. *Insha Allah.*" Al-Wahid turns away and closes the door forever on his eldest son.

The men in the outer room toast each other with one last round of goat's milk. The *mentor* speaks in a deep and deliberate voice, which undoubtedly can be heard by the prisoner on the other side of the wooden door: "My sincerest apologies for Tariq's ignorance and incompetence. He has disgraced us and cost our tribe dearly because of his failure to recognize and kill the American. And although we are now authorized to correct our error, it will not be possible for Tariq to correct his."

He continues, "But, esteemed brothers, be comforted in the knowledge that Allah has provided us with an opportunity to redeem our tribe's pride and respect. The vessel shall be another American. His name is Bobby Kennedy, and we shall not fail again."

The *mentor* turns both crystal bowls onto their sides, releasing the poisonous scorpions onto the table. He places both heavy Kosta Boda lead crystal bowls into his shoulder satchel and moves quickly toward to door.

As the men follow the *mentor* outdoors, one of them secures and padlocks the heavy wooden outer door. He then heaves the large wrought iron key into the air with all his strength. Some of the others, busy relieving themselves against the scrub bushes, watch as the black key spins end over end, almost as though in slow motion. When the key finally hits the ground, it disappears into a crevice in the rocky desert floor.

Mounting their respective beasts, each festooned with a different colored ribbon, the men head slowly back down the trail toward the coarse road leading back toward Khirbet An-Nbash and Damascus. One man trails slightly behind the caravan, followed by a riderless donkey on a long lead that, until only an hour ago, had sported a 7-1/2 millimeter-wide red ribbon around its neck.

Dark storm clouds are gathering in the western sky as the procession moves slowly, but purposely, toward the horizon and the city of Damascus beyond.

Unheard are the unrelenting screams of a young man left alone in excruciating pain and total darkness.

◄ Chapter 14 ►

Horatio and Elin Dine Fine in Stockholm's Old Town

SATURDAY, FEBRUARY 3, 1968

The American vice president and Elin Lindström arrive separately at the restaurant most Stockholmers consider to be the best of the many fine restaurants in Gamla Stan, the Old Town area of Stockholm. *Urgamlakällaren* is located at Brunnsgränd 2, not far from the Royal Palace.

A private taxi delivers Elin to the front door, where she's escorted down the right side of the unique elliptical-shaped double staircase which reminds her of a boulevard. At the bottom of the stairs is the original cellar of a building which was constructed in 1666 as a cold-storage food warehouse.

Elin is shown to a table already set for two. It's brightly decorated with an array of colorful spring flowers artfully placed in Orrefors vases blown in southern Sweden especially for Urgamlakällaren. Spring flowers in the middle of winter? How lovely!

The vice president, escorted by three U.S. Secret Service agents, arrives by car at the back of the restaurant. As per prearrangement, they enter through the seldom-used heavy wooden door leading to the rear emergency stairway. Humphrey's step is springy as he approaches the table and takes both of Elin's hands in his. He smiles as he gives her a small bouquet of fresh flowers, but refrains from kissing both her cheeks in the traditional European manner.

Elin, who had been speaking in Swedish to the maitre-d'hôtel, now turns her full attention to Horatio and thanks him both for the flowers and his kind words earlier regarding her late father. Sophisticated diners at nearby tables do seem a little distracted by the autumn/spring relationship that's playing out between Elin and the gentleman who seems faintly familiar from newspaper pictures.

———

Some years earlier, Humphrey had come to appreciate that in Sweden he is afforded the same respect for privacy and personal space that Swedes traditionally render to their own celebrities and politicians. Even though he doesn't sport a Swedish heritage, Vice President Humphrey is proud of his South Dakota roots, pharmaceutical education and subsequent Minnesota background and record of public service.

After spending most of his adult life working with and on behalf of Swedish immigrants in Minnesota and across America, Humphrey has earned the gratitude of Swedes on both sides of the Atlantic, who have adopted him as one of their own.

As if to meaningfully demonstrate his commitment and allegiance to both his American and Swedish friends and constituents, years earlier—after riding his first Harley-Davidson bike to Sturgis with some rough-and-tumble friends—Humphrey strolled into a nondescript tattoo parlor and asked the artist to sketch a special design and apply it to his chest. The result? Exactly midway between the vice president's tits is a six-inch-wide abstract design showing two elaborately entwined flags.

On the right is America's red, white and blue Old Glory, with a blue and yellow Swedish flag on the left. Later on he had second thoughts, thinking that a tattooed politician might seem to be a

less-than-serious curiosity. Thus, Humphrey stopped going swimming, and would remove his undershirt only to shower or to enjoy
a very private moment.

On more than one occasion, his longtime trusted friend,
Sweden's Prime Minister Tage Erlander, stated publicly that
Humphrey could easily be elected to high office in Sweden if
he worked on his language skills and became a Swedish citizen.

In the past, whenever the two leaders visited each other's
homes in a non-official capacity, nary a word was reported by the
American or Swedish press. Not even their mutual friend, Lars
Lindström, ever uttered a word in print about the private visits.

Nor did Lindström ever mention, except to a few trusted
friends, Vice President Humphrey's unplanned stop in 1965 at
the Lindström home on Lidingö. It followed his visit to nearby Millesgården to see Anne Hedmark, an old acquaintance of
Humphrey's who for many years had been the late Swedish
sculptor Carl Milles' assistant at the Cranbrook Art Academy
in Bloomfield Hills, Michigan. Miss Hedmark was later invited
to join Sweden's iconic sculptor and his wife when they moved
to Italy a few years before Milles' death in the early 1950s. She
now serves as curator of Stockholm's popular cultural attraction,
Millesgården, which is Milles' spacious home-turned-sculpture-
garden-and-museum.

———

Elin tells Humphrey that she has arranged the details of their
supper tonight. She explains that they are going to enjoy items
from a traditional Swedish smörgåsbord, which requires that the
food and accompaniments be served in a prescribed sequence.

"Now, dear Horatio, you may want to take some notes," she chides her supper partner. "The first round will be a variety of herring and dill sauce, while the second round consists of a variety of *cold* items. These are followed by the third and fourth rounds, which are served *hot*. Got that? And, of course, the last round is *dessert*, probably cheese followed by some fruit and sweet custard washed down with bracing coffee or tea."

"Your use of the word "rounds" makes me think you're describing a gourmet boxing match," he says. Once again, Elin doesn't understand Horatio's attempt at humor!

Now it's her turn. Elin smiles and winks as she says, "Perhaps I should have placed more emphasis on the word dessert." She hopes he got her double entendre!

After pouring the vice president aquavit from a bottle that has been frozen into a block of ice, she notes, "We won't be driving tonight, so it's okay for us to sip some alcohol." They sweetly toast each other with smiles and a few words followed by a customary Swedish skål, which Americans pronounce "skoal." Just in time, too, because the server is arriving with platters containing herring, cheeses and boiled new potatoes.

"Holy mackerel, Elin, you've arranged everything. It's so much more appetizing than I'm used to seeing back in Washington. Plus, here in Sweden there's no need to have a taster between me and my food!"

When Elin didn't understand his last remark, Humphrey tried to explain, tongue-in-cheek, that sometimes at higher levels of American society—as in czarist Russia—a personal food taster may be considered a requisite life-saving device.

———

Humphrey dramatically switches his conversation to a more serious tone. "Darn it, my darling, I've been meaning to ask you something. How's your new car working out?"

He laughs, "Is the paint red enough for you? And have you yet exceeded one hundred miles per hour? Probably not in Manhattan, eh? In any case, I'm sure you'll charm your way out of any speeding tickets."

Surprised by his comments, Elin hesitates before responding, "Why, Horatio," she purrs, "My Camaro convertible is absolutely marvelous. I mean, it's absolutely the best. I simply love it! And would you believe that a few of my friends call me the 'Ragtop Doll'? I like the name a lot. And it fits me, don't you think?"

She quickly adds, "But dear Horatio, like I've tried to tell you before, I do worry a little about you. I mean, what if somebody finds out? Wouldn't that be a problem?"

Humphrey again reassures Elin everything is okay. "I had Larry Gartner handle all aspects of the transaction for me, so as to keep the matter at 'arms length.' No government funds were involved. It's nobody else's business. And unless I fire Larry, he isn't going to spill the beans!"

Elin, who has never much liked Gartner and his uppity Middle-American know-it-all demeanor, seems comforted by the vice president's explanation and reassurance. She lets the matter drop.

———

Always talkative—frequently too much so for his own good—the vice president seems to be holding promise this evening of being even more loquacious than usual. Maybe it's the Swedish aquavit kicking in. Or maybe some of his old hormones are being jump-started.

In any case, he wants Elin to know that he, too, has a favorite "toy!" "Don't remember if I ever mentioned," Humphrey begins, "how much I miss my Harley-Davidson. Right now it's in the garage back in Waverly, and I'm itching to wring it out again at full speed."

He drones on, "It's a 1965 Electra-Guide, with the hand shifter on the tank. And the Holiday Red and White paint job is really visible! FLHB models like mine are popular with police departments, which usually order the hand shifter rather than a foot shifter. My bike's got a 74 cubic inch Panhead engine, plus an electric start and twelve-volt electrical system on a Big Twin. Its fitted with a five-gallon tank, and the tires are 5.00 x 16."

Realizing his words are starting to smother Elin, Humphrey switches topics and starts talking with unbridled candor about his almost daily confrontations back in Washington with President Johnson and certain folks over at the Defense and State Departments. Having now perked up, Elin listens attentively.

Not surprisingly, the main bone of contention back in the United States almost always involves the increasingly ugly and difficult-to-rationalize Vietnam War.

The vice president says he has long known that in Sweden his friend and liberal soulmate, Olof Palme, has become the Vietnam War's most outspoken critic. Palme's unrelenting harangues in various global forums have made him persona non grata in Washington. Few people of consequence back home realize that Humphrey and Palme not only are acquainted but have known each other since Palme headed up the University of Stockholm's student legislature.

Hawks at the Pentagon and in the CIA are constantly prying into Palme's personal life in an attempt to find something they can use to compromise Palme's venom toward President Johnson and America's war machine. So far, nothing particularly harmful has appeared in the U.S. press. But Hubert Humphrey figures it's just a matter of time!

Humphrey does suspect, however, that word of his close relationship with Palme may have reached LBJ and unwittingly created a chasm in Vice President Humphrey's delicate relationship with his boss in the White House.

———

Instead of the romantic table talk that Elin was anticipating, her Horatio tilts the conversation toward the anticipated nomination fight at this coming August's Democratic National Convention in Chicago. Of particular interest to him is the expected candidacy of Robert F. Kennedy, brother of the martyred JFK.

Vice President Humphrey says that the U.S. government's intelligence community has been developing G2 intelligence on a group of young American ultra-radicals. He smilingly describes them as "the type of revolutionary I wanted to be, except most of them woefully lack my charm and charisma." Horatio studies Elin's face to see if she gets his little joke. She hasn't!

It's evident that Humphrey particularly admires the leadership skills of a former University of Michigan student activist and civil-rights protester from Port Huron named Tom Hayden. During his college days in Ann Arbor, young Hayden had founded SDS, Students for a Democratic Society.

Humphrey tells Elin that authorities are convinced that Hayden and his band of budding revolutionaries plan to try upstaging the convention with a series of mass demonstrations on the streets of Chicago. "At this point," says Humphrey, "the authorities say it's impossible to predict how bad things might get!"

The vice president tells Elin of another nagging concern he hasn't mentioned before. It's about the campaign war chest that Bobby Kennedy has already amassed. "From what I hear, they've accumulated enough money to actually buy RFK the election should he pick up the Dems' nomination in Chicago. It's happened before, and it's a scary thought!

"Indeed, it could be a repeat of what his brother did in 1960," Humphrey says. Although he doubts that the younger Kennedy will earn the Democrat's nomination, it's a matter that's costing key Democratic strategists some restless nights.

———

The vice president tells Elin that he's begun to question the loyalty of his key aide, Lawrence Gartner. "I'm convinced Larry's got some sort of hidden agenda and honestly, I don't know what he may be up to. It's no surprise to me that Gartner's an opportunist. Otherwise, why would he be involved with national politics?"

"I've long figured it's a useful trait in an aide-de-camp. But now I think Larry is probably more liberal than me, and that he dreams of one day playing a pivotal role in transforming America into a society modeled on Sweden's traditional socialist system. Let's call it the original 'Swedish model' . . . although I think Larry's version may be more functional than pretty to look at!"

Humphrey smiles at his clever wordplay. Once again, Elin doesn't get it. Although her English comprehension is good, once in a while the vice president's use of the language is so subtle it goes over her head . . . as it often goes over the head of many folks back in Washington!

He resists letting go of the topic. "You know, Sweetnips, unless somebody reels in Larry's ambition, I think someday he might actually seek control of a major American television network news operation. You know, like NBC News, or maybe CBS or ABC. That way, at least to Larry's way of thinking, he could wield significant influence over American public opinion all day long and all night long, every single day of the year. What a wonderful aphrodisiac for a wannabe power monger!"

"Yes, Elin, the more I think about it, the more I'm convinced that's the reason Larry is spending so much time these days trying to cozy up to Andy Ryan in D.C. Gartner knows that Ryan's law firm is number one in the communications, energy and space sectors. Most importantly, he knows that Ryan handles both NBC's legal affairs and all of LBJ's broadcast interests back in Texas. Guess we'll just have to wait and see how it all plays out!"

———

Once again the dining table, still fresh looking with its fine white linen tablecloth, is being cleared. "Well, now it's time to enjoy some hot dishes."

The vice president can't recall when he's seen so many different foods on the same table at one time. Rare roast beef, pork tenderloin stuffed with prunes, liver pâté, veal with parsley butter, Jansson's Temptation, beef à la Lindström, Swedish meatballs. And, Jesus Christ, there's more!

———

As the food is being served, Elin finally succeeds in redirecting the conversation toward herself . . . and her photography projects, her FLUXUS art projects and her friends in Manhattan. She grins, "Let's talk about me for a moment."

Elin reminds Horatio about her days at Georgetown University and the core group of school friends with whom she bonded early on . . . especially the amalgam of Arab and Israeli students with whom she enjoyed sharing time and experiences.

"It's true," Elin says, "that I probably gravitated toward the Middle Eastern crowd because of Papa's intense interest in that region of the world. Of course, we lived there for a few years, and I've always been fascinated by the area's unrelenting reputation as a source of surprise, mystery and intrigue."

Quite honestly, Humphrey is more interested in hearing about Elin's art, so, he interrupts her with, "I mean, what is this FLUXUS art stuff really all about?"

She hesitates a moment while her mind tries to refocus on his question. "Horatio, let me tell you a little secret that you Washington types don't know about. And I know what I'm talking about, because I lived in D.C. during school at Georgetown and afterwards.

While understanding that FLUXUS art probably is undefinable, Elin decides to jump in and attempt the impossible. "Now listen up, my privileged friend who has lived such a sheltered life. FLUXUS is all about having wit, little or no money, sincerity, an idea about art, a sense of 'game' and gamesmanship, and humanity."

Smiling, she asks, "Are you paying attention, Horatio? Honestly, do you even have a clue as to what I'm saying?"

He responds, "This FLUXUS stuff sounds far too complicated to be art. To me, art is something that goes on a wall, maybe to cover up a nail pop. Sorry I asked."

"No, no, you aren't. You're not really sorry, darling! You're not going to get out of it that easily," teases Elin. "Now you just listen up for a moment. You asked me, and now I'm going to tell you!

"FLUXUS art isn't a complex concept at all. For me, FLUXUS can pretty much be defined as 'the art of the insignificant.' Now that's easy to understand, isn't it?

"For example, Horatio, remember last year when I sent you some color snapshots showing various scenes around the world . . . each including those large bright yellow signs I had printed up. You know the pictures . . . the ones with yellow signs that say *'Posted! No Hunting, Fishing Or FLUXUS Permitted. Violators Will Be Persecuted'.*"

America's vice president stares blankly at his tablemate. *What the hell is the lady talking about?*

"Oh well, it doesn't matter," Elin sighs, "I guess you forgot. Or maybe you didn't even see them. You certainly would have remembered them because each photo was taken of a landmark in a different place—like Geneva, Stockholm, Tel Aviv, Manhattan, Tokyo, São Paulo—with a yellow 'Posted!' notice strategically placed in each picture.

"I'd swear that I mailed you photos taken in several different places. Like outside of the front gate at the U.S.S.R. Embassy in Geneva. In that shot, I pinned the sign on the back of an old man wearing a long brown cloth coat before positioning him facing the big black iron gates.

"Other pics showed that funky and really creative Shifrin ad agency in Tel Aviv, the Little Mermaid on the water in Copenhagen, Paris' Eiffel Tower, the Van Gogh Museum in Amsterdam and a marvelous sumo wrestling palace in Tokyo. My friends think the photographs are, to use an American expression, 'a bit of a hoot'!

"I even think I sent you a copy of my personal favorite, taken right here in Stockholm. It's the one with the 'Posted!' notice tacked on the front door of the quirky Museum of House Painting.

"You know, Horatio, Manhattan is the best showcase anywhere for FLUXUS art. There you'll find the likes of John Cage, Alison Knowles, Dick Higgins. And, of course, George Brecht, George Macuinas and Yoko Ono, who's really on a roll these days."

Elin continues, "You'll like Brecht, and I'll try to introduce you next time you're in Manhattan. I love his philosophy because it's so simple and straightforward. Brecht says that each of us has our own ideas about what FLUXUS is all about . . . and so much the better. That way, it'll take longer to bury the movement!

"But for me," Elin continues, "FLUXUS is a community of individuals who get along with each other, and who are interested in each others' work and personality. To me, that's what FLUXUS is all about!"

The vice president picks at some pickled onions and creamed potatoes, and mumbles, "I've never seen so many different kinds of potatoes."

Elin shakes her pretty head. "I honestly believe that my FLUXUS art activities put people at ease . . . and *that*, in turn, permits me to do my other more important projects without raising undue ire or suspicion."

Speaking with utter candor, she says, "FLUXUS and my photography provide an ideal *cover* for the things I do for you, Horatio. So you shouldn't be overly critical!" Each smiles knowingly at the other.

———

Elin notices a gentleman sitting with a male friend two tables away. It's an old acquaintance, Stockholm ad executive Håkan Verner-Carlsson. They exchange discreet little hand waves. Before long, Verner-Carlsson sends a bottle of fine Madeira to the table occupied by Elin Lindström and her friend.

———

Minutes later, the blissful couple agree they've had far too much to eat and drink. It's almost too easy for them to decide they'll take a pass on rich dessert and strong Swedish coffee.

Elin says, "I have a better idea, Horatio. Let's walk off some of our calories. And then," she teases, "Maybe, my dear, that'll put you in the mood for a little chilled Swedish Punch before I serve-up your favorite Swedish dessert."

The vice president again smiles, winks and gently squeezes her hand across the table.

———

Humphrey's principle security man takes care of paying for the dinner and leaves an additional gratuity that's sure to be remembered.

Helping Elin into her coat, Vice President Humphrey leads her along the back hallway, up the rear stairwell and then out the back door into the crisp February night air.

Trailing behind at a discreet distance are two of the three U.S. Secret Service agents Elin had seen earlier in the funeral procession. The third agent is busy telephoning the American Embassy with yet another update on their client's location and activities. The agent is heard to say "Well, team, this could be an early evening . . . or a long night!"

Like it or not, the vice president's security team realizes that this week's murder in front of the Grand Hotel has probably signaled a sea change in traditional Swedish life and values. It seems apparent that people in Sweden are no longer immune to the kinds of dangers long prevalent in many parts of the world, but ignored far too long by Swedish authorities.

Many citizens believe that Swedish politicians have been unwilling to modify national policies that permit easy entry into Sweden by immigrants who have little respect nor appreciation for the importance of traditional Swedish culture and values, common courtesy, decency and the language. In Sweden, taking advantage of the system is becoming the norm rather than an exception!

Both Elin and Horatio recognize that, far too often, it's the pushy outsiders who have not earned their own way who are able to win and live off of the government's largess. Meanwhile, Sweden's elderly and truly needy frequently have to go with less, or without. Sad to say, every day Sweden is becoming more like Vice President Humphrey's America.

It may not be long before some *crazy* shows up to demonstrate the proposition that, in modern Sweden, the odds of getting your way improve dramatically when a gun barrel is introduced into the equation.

◄ Chapter 15 ►

A Romantic Late-Night Stroll Along
Gamla Stan's Sparkling Wintry Streets

SATURDAY, FEBRUARY 3, 1968

The February night air is brisk and refreshing, and the wind that whipped the Swedish flags earlier in the day has blown east out over the Baltic. Only a hint of snow remains on the ground in the central city.

Elin thinks to herself, *It's like morning two days ago when I was driving over the 59th Street Bridge into Manhattan.* She stops dead in her tracks and squeezes her companion's hand.

"Horatio, so much has happened during just the past two days! I'm past exhaustion." He folds his arms around her as she begins to weep.

The uneven, well-worn cobblestones glisten in the halo of the ornate two-hundred year-old wrought iron gas lamps that long ago were converted to electricity. Although the cobblestones look slippery, they're actually dry.

Elin wishes she had thought to slip a more comfortable pair of shoes into her large black leather satchel. *So many details, so little time,* she thinks to herself.

Humphrey's security detail, which at first seemed a little tense with Elin around, is now relieved and probably not surprised by the total lack of attention the two friends draw as they stroll arm-in-arm east along Brunnsgränd toward Skeppsbron.

Twice along the way, Elin points out elegant old buildings

in which her attorney friend, Hans Belfrage, owns illegal apartments. "You see," she says, "a person can't own more than one apartment in the Gamla Stan area of Stockholm. I suspect Hans' legal clients may sometimes pay him with apartments instead of money!"

She dredges up her recollection of a late-evening incident from a few years earlier, told to her by Alec Ramsay. She explains how that particular evening has become known among a few mutual friends as "Hans' and Alec's Midnight Madness Travail."

"I think it was in 1963," she says, "when Alec Ramsay helped Hans Belfrage empty out the apartment of a Belfrage tenant who was hopelessly and shamelessly behind in his rent. Between midnight and 1:30 a.m., they lugged all of the poor guy's furniture and possessions down four flights of stairs.

"As the guys were completing their 'midnight-mission', a locksmith previously hired by Belfrage was upstairs changing the door locks on the now-empty apartment. Even at triple overtime, Belgrage knew it was well worth the effort!

"Everything was neatly piled on the sidewalk next to the curb. With their task finished, Belfrage strolled back to his own apartment and Ramsay took a taxi to the Strand Hotel."

———

Suddenly, Elin again stops dead in her tracks and turns toward the vice president. She says, "Wanna know one of my sweetest dreams, Horatio?"

Not waiting for his response, she continues, "It's that someday there will be two streets here in Gamla Stan named after men I love."

Humphrey pauses for a moment and then volunteers, "I'd

guess that one will be called LarsLindströmgätan. And what would be the second one be called, my darling?"

"Silly you! How does Horatiogätan sound?" she whispers into the crisp night air. "Now don't tell me you're surprised."

"Well, it does have a certain unique ring. But tell me, will I have to die first?"

Realizing immediately the enormity and absolute insensitivity of his remark, the vice president says quietly, "I apologize, my love. I'm really so sorry for that one."

Elin turns her head ever so slightly, purses her lip and says, "Not a problem."

———

At the pier along the east side of Skeppsbron, and adjacent to a large empty and unlit parking lot, they gingerly board an enclosed motor launch that quickly and quietly takes them the few hundred meters or so across the ferry channel to Kurt-Visby Rädisson's yacht.

From the Strommen side, or water side, of the yacht they scramble up a movable stairway. It's out of the view of any eyes that may still be awake and watching from the Grand Hotel side . . . or maybe even along the Strömkajen promenade.

Elin assumes that the launch also belongs to Mr. Rädisson, although she's not sure. But she doesn't ask. What she does know is that the skipper and crew members are wearing the same odd-shaped lapel buttons that identify U.S. Secret Service agents as members of America's third most exclusive fraternity.

Elin recalls once hearing Alec Ramsay mention that there are probably two groups tied for first place as the most exclusive in America. "Like they say, one is the U.S. Senate," said Ramsay.

"And the other one?" she asked. "It's Delta Kappa Epsilon, of course." Known as the Greek Peak, the huge three-story DEKE house out on Geddes Road in Ann Arbor had spawned both Andy Ryan, Jr. and Alec Ramsay during the late '50s.

Years before, at Yale University in New Haven, DEKE's exclusivity and principles had helped to cultivate, motivate and launch the career of Texas' newest U.S. Congressman, George Herbert Walker Bush. Raised in Connecticut as the son of a senior U.S. senator, Congressman Bush is an entrepreneurial oil man from Texas who one day may himself aspire to become a U.S. senator.

◄ Chapter 16 ►

Berthing Down, So To Speak,
Aboard Kurt-Visby Rädisson's Yacht

SATURDAY, FEBRUARY 3, 1968

Kurt-Visby Rädisson's sleek 232-foot yacht, *World Class,* was built by the German shipbuilder Lürssen. Before the first sheet of steel was cut and shaped for the hull, project coordinators spent four years performing extensive model tests to ensure that every one of the owner's and the captain's mandates for speed and stability would be met.

The yacht has a full-time crew responsible for moving the craft between ports in accordance with Mr. Rädisson's wishes. Although its home base is in Monte Carlo, the yacht frequently visits ports in Bermuda, Sweden and the Caribbean. Crew members hail from England, Australia, South Africa, Sweden, the Netherlands and the United States.

Vice President Humphrey, a frequent guest aboard *World Class,* chooses not to give Elin a full tour tonight. At least not of the vessel! Instead, he gently grasps Elin's left hand and leads her toward his stateroom.

As they pad along the richly carpeted corridor, Humphrey explains that Rädisson is a longtime friend and supporter from Minneapolis who made a fortune selling retail trading stamps.

"They're called Value Stamps, and food shoppers collect and paste them into special stamp books that can be redeemed for various kinds of merchandise.

"He and I have an informal arrangement that works well for both of us. Simply put, Kurt-Visby gives me money, and I help him attain access to people and officials in the United States and elsewhere. These are people who can assist him in achieving his dream of owning significantly more than his share of the world.

"I think Kurt-Visby wants to be like Ian Fleming's *Goldfinger*, but without the rough edges!"

Humphrey laughingly continues, "I don't mean to exaggerate when I tell you Kurt-Visby is ambitious. I tell him that he'll be satisfied only when these words can be carved into his Swedish granite tombstone that sits waiting for him in a Minneapolis suburb: 'Here Rests America's Richest Swede.' Kurt-Visby insists that he simply won't die before that happens!"

Elin gasps as they step into the stateroom, which is a showcase of beautifully crafted Cuban mahogany nicely offset by grooved white oak paneling overhead, with recessed lighting.

———

Since they were introduced in early 1963, Vice President Humphrey and Elin have forged an almost magical bond that's buttressed by mutual trust. Once again, that word *trust*. It means a lot to both of them.

Otherwise, why would either of them—and most especially Humphrey, arguably the second most powerful politician in America—risk everything by taking the chances they do? They've been together in Washington, Paris, Amman, once in California and now in Sweden.

The risks they take are part of what, at least for them, makes life stimulating and worth living!

———

Basking in a cocoon of soft background music and gentle vocals by Johnny Mathis and Frank Sinatra, the couple share a snifter of icy cold Swedish Punch and more small-talk about the upcoming campaign back in the States. Elin knows that Humphrey is aware that 1968 may be his only chance to run for the U.S. presidency. Somehow he needs to figure out how to survive Bobby Kennedy's expected onslaught.

Like a Burroughs mainframe computer, Humphrey ticks off the pros and cons that each potential Democrat contender will need to consider when taking on Nixon. He seems confident that the Republicans will nominate Nixon rather than Nelson Rockefeller or George Romney, despite Nixon's lack of executive experience.

———

Slow-dancing in lazy circles while alternating sips of Swedish Punch with extra-tender caresses, Elin gently steers Humphrey onto the huge bed and into a romantic interlude. It's the dessert that she promised him back at the restaurant. And it's sweeter than ever.

On this night, Elin intends to help Horatio eliminate any lingering self-doubt he may have regarding his ability and capacity to perform in a manner that can delight both of them.

Elin believes it's important to reinforce, through vigorous sex, the vice president's positive self-image as a whole man. While it may not lead directly to peace in the Middle East, she sees good sex as a means of demonstrating to each other an appreciation for perpetual high energy, youthful enthusiasm, overachievement and a general zest for life.

With lights in the stateroom dimmed, and the sounds of a little-known group from Stockholm named the Hootenanny Singers rocking quietly with the gentle roll of the yacht moored in the harbor, Horatio and Elin warmly embrace.

Their king-sized berth is wide enough, deep enough and sturdy enough to envelop their bodies as they physically and spiritually soar out of control. With his eyes closed to reality, Horatio can't believe his good fortune.

Elin has already left behind the tragedy that brought them together again.

The vice president looks rather silly with his grey and white striped boxers, dark socks, faded six inch flag tattoo on his chest and fleshy, out-of-condition potbelly. He reaches into his right sock and pulls out a blue plastic 4-X capsule.

Using his right thumb and forefinger, he applies pressure on the capsule until he feels the subtle "crack" as the two halves of the tiny container break apart. In hand rests one "genuine and pre-moistened" sheepskin prophylactic. Humphrey places it alongside his pillow. This brand of translucent sheepskin is promoted as "the ultimate protection against pregnancy and disease."

The vice president places both hands on Elin's full breasts and gently massages her nipples. One hand is slightly moist after being warmed between his thighs.

"I love you, Sweetnips," he murmurs. Given the setting and moment, Horatio's use of this nickname seems a little crude and unnecessary.

Feeling her nipples stiffen even more, the vice president lets one hand touch Elin's knee and then slowly brush upward toward her vagina. His fingers tell him that her warm moist opening somehow seems larger now than when they were last together.

For an old guy out-of-training, I ain't doing so badly, he muses to himself.

Vice President Humphrey submits to the slight pressure on his head as Elin's left hand eases his face across her breasts and down toward her midsection. The vice president's tongue is operating in overdrive, moving quickly in and out like a snake frantically trying to find its way home. But now is hardly the time to over-intellectualize, to paint crazy pictures in the mind.

Ecstasy! Elin exhales, moaning uncontrollably, and her body shudders at the magic of the moment when her Horatio's tongue hits pay dirt.

Coming up for air, Humphrey reaches for the sheepskin and slips it easily over a member that is standing proudly at attention, straighter and firmer than any U.S. Marine corpsman guarding the Tomb of the Unknown Soldier at Arlington Cemetery.

Slowly they roll over, and Elin mounts Horatio.

Again, there's an overpowering emotional release. It's rapturous delight, the frenzy of sensual inspiration, dreams and accomplishment.

After resting for a few moments, almost totally spent, Elin gently rises up and carefully removes the prophylactic from Horatio's collapsed member. His eyes open momentarily and he smiles weakly, lovingly.

Elin leans over to lick, kiss, and caress the vice president's Swedish meatballs.

She then kisses his right cheek before sliding off of the lavender-colored silk bed sheets and into the adjacent bathroom where she flips on the light and closes the door behind her.

She knows precisely what to do with the contents of the sheepskin dangling limply in her left hand.

◄ Chapter 17 ►

*1968 Already is Crammed with Enough Turmoil to
Make Many Americans Wonder if November's
Presidential Election Will Happen*

FEBRUARY 4 THROUGH MARCH 4, 1968

Clearly, 1968 already is turning into the year many Americans and their leaders want to forget.

It can be surmised that citizens and leaders alike are trying to sort out the reasons behind all the headlines. Nobody seems to have answers, nor even a broad-brush vision of what will be required to diffuse myriad problems that are plaguing America and the world.

On one hand, President Lyndon Johnson asserts in early February that the Communist offensive in South Vietnam is "a complete failure." Both he and his defense secretary, Robert McNamara, seemingly will never admit their own failures.

On February 7, at the second United Nations Conference on Trade and Development, nearly all Arab and African delegates walk out as the Israeli delegate rises to address the conference. It's quite obvious that any progress made during the previous week's Middle East peace conference in Stockholm hasn't carried over to folks involved in the U.N. conference.

The next day, former Alabama Governor George Wallace announces his third party presidential candidacy. On the same day, Massachusetts Senator Robert Kennedy calls for political compromise in Vietnam since, he says, "a total military victory is not within sight." President Johnson is angry all day, while Vice

President Humphrey keeps his head down and tries to stay out of sight. Both believe that Defense Secretary McNamara is growing weary and will soon announce his resignation.

A week later, a Gallup Poll reports public approval of President Johnson's handling of the war has declined to 35 percent. Israeli Premier Levi Eshkol warns Jordan about artillery attacks on Israeli forces, while the United States announces that it will resume arms shipments to Jordan. And Arab guerrilla group El Fatah ignores Jordanian King Hussein's February 16 warning not to use Jordan as a guerrilla base.

Still in February, Jerusalem Mayor Teddy Kollek complains that Israeli efforts to integrate the Arab and Jewish sections of Jerusalem socially and psychologically have been a "total failure."

Black Power advocates H. Rap Brown and Stokely Carmichael address rallies in California, and on February 20 police arrest H. Rap Brown in New York.

On February 21, a bomb explodes at the Soviet Embassy in Washington, D.C., just across from Andrew Gallagher Ryan's home on 16th Street.

The same day, Swedish Education Minister Olof Palme leads an anti-Vietnam War demonstration in Stockholm. President Johnson is fit to be tied, and appeals to Vice President Humphrey to intercede with Palme. Humphrey says he'll try, but doesn't think it'll do any good!

U.S. Senate Democratic leader Mike Mansfield leaves a meeting at Andrew Gallagher Ryan's home and immediately calls a press conference in which he calls for the halt of the bombing of North Vietnam. President Johnson grows ever more frustrated. Vice President Humphrey continues to stay out of sight!

On March 1, Clark Clifford is sworn in as the new U.S. Defense Secretary, replacing Robert McNamara, who had been on the job since JFK hired him away from Ford Motor Company.

By March 3, Israeli authorities have destroyed yet another family residence of a suspected Arab guerrilla leader in Jerusalem. Jerusalem Mayor Teddy Kollek, an Israeli, joins other protesters in criticizing the Israelis for extending to East Jerusalem their military practice of blowing up the home of suspected Arab guerrillas. Israeli General Ariel Sharon tells Kollek to "shut up and go to hell!"

Vice President Hubert Humphrey is quoted on March 4 as saying that the president's National Advisory Commission on Civil Disorders' March 3 warning that the United States is moving toward two "separate and unequal" societies is "open to some challenge."

To counter Humphrey's statement, a pastoral letter is read at all the masses in St. Patrick's Cathedral in Manhattan to support the March 3 conclusions of the president's National Advisory Commission blaming "white racism" as the underlying cause of racial riots.

◄ Chapter 18 ►

Another Early Morning in Mr. Treleavan's Office at J. Walter Thompson

TUESDAY, MARCH 5, 1968

Even though dawn is only just now peeking over the horizon, Harry Treleavan is in his office and ringing Alec Ramsay's apartment on East 60th.

"Good morning Alexander. It's Harry. Excuse my early call, but we need to cover a couple of things right away."

Must be bad news coming, Alec figures, because when Treleavan calls him Alexander, Ramsay knows something serious is bound to follow. *He thinks like my mother!*

"First off, maybe you saw that Vice President Humphrey was quoted yesterday as saying 'the president's National Advisory Commission on Civil Disorders warning that the United States is moving toward two separate and unequal societies is open to some challenge.' See what you can find out about what Humphrey means when he says 'open to some challenge.'"

Treleavan continues, "And the other thing—and this is really important—we have it on highly reliable authority that Humphrey is playing hanky-panky again with your friend, Miss . . . ah, what's her name? It's not Lindberg . . . it's, ah, yes, Lindström! And, for chrissakes, they've been doin' it in Sweden, of all places. And his timing is astoundingly poor. I mean, think about it, man. Her dad's body isn't even cold yet, and this clown is probably trying to hump her bones. We can't be locked-tight sure about this yet . . .

but, Jesus Christ Almighty, he needs to get a fucking life!"

"Well, Harry," Ramsay retorts, "I certainly haven't heard anything. But you can't deny that Vice President Humphrey has had some impressive political role models." Alec continues, "Judging by what we've been hearing about Johnson, Kennedy, Eisenhower and Roosevelt, maybe it's the lead residue in the paint and drinking water at the White House that causes it. Actually, you gotta exclude Eisenhower because he was caught pin-cushioning his driver—or whatever he called her—during the Second World War—long before Ike was tapped to be president of Columbia University and then the United States of America."

"Between you and me, Alec," Treleavan retorts, "I kinda hope that Humphrey did get something, 'cause I can't imagine him scoring anything at home. Ya know, I actually feel kinda sorry for the geezer." He hesitates a moment to contemplate his next step.

"Quite honestly," says Harry, "I don't think we can get much mileage out of this deal right now. Certainly it's nothing to bother Big John about." Ultimately, this snap decision by Harry Treleavan may turn out to be one of the 1968 campaign's worst.

"One thing's for sure," says Treleavan, "I can't picture Richard Nixon ever getting his weeny stuck in some broad. He's way too smart, calculating and emotionally void. Our guy's passion is strictly politics, not cheap sex. And certainly not expensive sex!"

Treleavan and Ramsay move on to a few other matters before hanging up. Treleavan tells Alec to make a note that Martin Luther King, Jr. has announced that his "nonviolent Poor People's March on Washington" will begin April 22. He also asks Ramsay to find out about the odds of Vice President Humphrey becoming the Democratic nominee, should President Johnson decide not to run. Treleavan still doesn't realize there's a DNC tap on his phone.

◄ Chapter 19 ►

1968 Continues Overloaded with Trouble and Unpredictability

MARCH 14 THROUGH MARCH 31, 1968

On March 14, Senator Robert Kennedy says that he cannot support President Johnson for renomination. Then, on March 16, Bobby Kennedy announces his candidacy for the Democratic presidential nomination.

RFK's announcement, combined with extremely contentious anti-war sentiments being expressed by Senate Majority Leader Mike Mansfield, JFK's former chief aide McGeorge Bundy and Swedish Premier Tage Erlander, is causing President Johnson to figuratively barricade himself in the White House. There is actually concern being expressed regarding the state of Johnson's mental health.

By March 16, President Johnson is telling the press that if the Communists refuse to negotiate in Vietnam then "we shall win a settlement on the battlefield."

Ironically, also on March 16 in Vietnam, the My Lai Massacre is carried out by U.S. troops under the command of Detroit's Lt. William L. Calley, Jr.

On March 17, the day after announcing that he's running for president, Senator Robert Kennedy says he would have "great reservations" about supporting President Johnson if the Democrats renominate him.

On the morning of March 18, Senator Kennedy opens his

presidential campaign with a stinging attack on President Johnson's Vietnam policy. He concedes his share of the responsibility for initial U.S. policy in Vietnam in the early 1960s, but adds that "past error is no excuse for its own perpetuation."

By that afternoon, President Johnson calls for "a total national effort" to win the Vietnam War.

The next day, March 19, Jordanian Ambassador to the United Nations, Mohammed Al-Farra charges that Israel is contemplating a massive thrust into Jordan. Two days later, fifteen thousand Israeli troops carry out a day-long raid in Jordan.

Also on March 19, Senators Robert Kennedy and Eugene McCarthy agree to run a joint anti-war slate in Washington, D.C. Many American boys continue to go north to Canada to escape the draft. And France grants residence and work permits to five U.S. Army deserters.

New York Governor Nelson Rockefeller announces on March 21 that he will *not* campaign "directly or indirectly for the U.S. presidency."

Jordanian King Hussein declares that his government is not responsible for the security of Israel, and therefore will do nothing to inhibit guerrillas operating from Jordan.

HEW Department Secretary nominee Wilbur Cohen says that the vast majority of Americans on welfare are incapable of doing the most elementary work tasks.

On March 24, a survey by *The New York Times* indicates that President Johnson could win 65 percent of the votes at the August Democratic National Convention in Chicago.

The next day, March 25, Maryland's General Assembly approves a bill liberalizing conditions under which abortion is legal. The same day, Senator Eugene McCarthy reverses himself by withdrawing from his March 19 agreement to run a joint slate of delegates in Washington, D.C., with Senator Robert Kennedy.

In response, Senator Robert Kennedy says that "each person has to examine his own conscience and do what he thinks is right" when faced with the prospect of military service in Vietnam.

Martin Luther King, Jr. says on March 26 that his projected march on Washington, D.C., will include the construction of "a shanty town." President Johnson instructs Vice President Humphrey to tell King to cancel his plans for the massive march. Humphrey demurs, reinforcing Johnson's view that his number two is disloyal.

Problems in 1968 aren't limited to America, because on March 27 Soviet Colonel Yuri Gagarin, the first man to make an orbital flight, dies in a jet plane crash.

An Associated Press survey released the same day reveals that fourteen of twenty-four Democratic governors favor President Johnson while only two are leaning toward Senators Kennedy or McCarthy. Fortunately for Vice President Humphrey, his name is not mentioned in the press.

On March 28, Senator Robert Kennedy criticizes former Vice President Richard Nixon's proposals for dealing with the Vietnam War on the grounds that they offer no change from current policies. He also declares that in America, "there is 'a double standard' for U.S. health care which benefits the wealthy." It's obvious that Kennedy is expanding his personal "war" against potential candidates for the 1968 presidency.

Another international conference is held in Stockholm. On March 30, nine of the ten leading financial nations (with France in dissent) endorse a plan to create a new form of monetary reserves to supplement gold, dollars and pounds. It's unclear if there's a coincidence when, on the same day, Czechoslovakia asks for the return of the gold taken out of its territory by the retreating

Germans in World War II, which was then confiscated by the United States.

All hell is threatening to break out as March ends. Bowie State College students in Maryland seize the administrative building on their campus. Several hundred demonstrators march in support of striking sanitation workers in Memphis, Tennessee.

A Gallup Poll says that the public's approval of President Johnson's performance is at a record low 36 percent.

On March 31, 1968, President Johnson announces, "I shall not seek and I will not accept the nomination of my party for another term as your president." He also says that he has unilaterally ordered a bombing halt of North Vietnam except for the territory just above the demilitarized zone.

◄ Chapter 20 ►

Politics Writer Tom Wicker's Office at The New York Times

SUNDAY, MARCH 31, 1968

"Son of a bitch," mutters Tom Wicker, top political writer at *The New York Times*.

It's early Sunday evening and all Wicker wants to do is go home and chill out after another harrowing week. The prospect of a hot shower and then bed seems exciting. Wicker has already filed his story for the next morning's paper when the phone rings. The call is from President Johnson's Washington lawyer, Andrew Gallagher Ryan.

"Tom, are you sitting down?" Ryan asks in a surprisingly quiet voice. Wicker thinks Ryan's voice is measured and controlled compared to the usual stentorian baritone punctuated with verbal accent marks that surely must derive from Ryan's Irish heritage and training as a lawyer.

"What's up, Andy?" replies Wicker.

"Look, Lyndon is going to issue a statement in a few minutes that is going to shock the nation," said Ryan, "and I need for you to get it exactly right."

"Shit, Andy, what the hell are you talking about? Are you off the wagon again?" Wicker knew he could get away talking this way to his old friend Ryan because it was one Irishman talking profanely to another.

The fact is, Wicker knows Ryan well enough to know that

taking a drink or two on the Lord's Day is never considered inappropriate. And most certainly not for Ryan, who once used his briefcase to smuggle a bottle of fine Irish whiskey into the Vatican along with four Irish crystal goblets. When two aides ushered Ryan into the pope's quarters, Ryan calmly poured drinks for himself, the pope and both aides!

Ryan later claimed that his meeting with Pope Pius XII went far more smoothly because of the lubrication. "And after all," he said, "what was the worst that could happen? They certainly weren't going to toss me out, not if they wanted my help in funding the new cathedral in Washington, D.C."

"Andy," Wicker finally said, "what the hell's going on? Why are you keeping me from going home to a warm shower, some hot soup and a firm bed with a warm, freshly moisturized body waiting for me?"

"Because," Ryan confides, "the president is going to announce tonight that he'll *not* run for re-election!"

"Holy crap, Andy! Does this mean that Humphrey will take on Bobby Kennedy?"

There was no answer. Only the click of Ryan hanging up his telephone!

◄ Chapter 21 ►

Breaking News and Events Threaten to Make November's Election Superfluous

APRIL 1 THROUGH MAY 12, 1968

On the first day of April, U.S. Senators Robert Kennedy and Eugene McCarthy praise President Johnson's decision to restrict the bombing of North Vietnam. As they are speaking, U.S. air strikes against North Vietnam range as far as 205 miles north of the demilitarized zone.

Senator McCarthy, who on April 2 wins the Wisconsin Democratic primary with 57.6 percent of the vote, says that he has asked Democratic leaders not to make commitments to a presidential candidate until later in the campaign.

Senator Robert Kennedy says on April 2, not surprisingly, that the United States should re-examine its entire position in Vietnam. The same day, Secretary of State Dean Rusk states his opposition to a coalition government in South Vietnam.

French President Charles de Gaulle on April 3 hails President Johnson's decision to limit the bombing of North Vietnam. And North Vietnam and the United States agree to establish direct diplomatic contact.

But the biggest surprise of all on April 3 is the White House meeting between President Johnson and Senator Robert Kennedy. Less surprising is MGM's release in New York City of Stanley Kubrick's movie entitled *2001: A Space Odyssey*.

April 4 is filled with terrible news: *An assassin kills the Rev.*

Martin Luther King, Jr. in Memphis, Tennessee.

Racial disorders break out on April 5 in major U.S. cities in the wake of Martin Luther King's assassination. And France agrees to sell Iraq fifty-four Mirage fighter-bombers.

The Canadian Liberal Party elects Justice Minister Pierre Elliott Trudeau as its leader on April 6.

In Brazil, Bishop Jose Castro Pinto and fourteen priests issue a statement critical of the ruling military regime headed by General Castello-Branco.

Racial disorders rock Washington, D.C., and Chicago, while the U.S. Commander in Vietnam, General William Westmoreland, confers with President Johnson at the White House.

On April 7, twelve Negro students hold Tuskegee Institute trustees captive for several hours to protest their refusal to adopt students' demands for reform. In a joint communiqué on the same day, the Soviet Union and Iran express similar views regarding Middle Eastern, Southeast Asian and European security.

The next day, April 8, several dozen Israeli helicopter-borne soldiers cross eighteen miles into Jordan in pursuit of Arab guerrillas. At the same time, Egyptian President Nasser discounts the possibility of talks with Israel. In fact, Egypt declares its full support of the Palestinian resistance movement.

On the same day, racial disorders hit Cincinnati, Pittsburgh and Nashville, and Kansas City braces for more of the same.

Iraq announces its rejection of foreign bids to develop its sulphur deposits and the North Rumaila oil fields.

On April 10, Swiss counter-FLUXUS art historian Sigfried Giedion dies in Zurich at age seventy-nine, which is viewed as positive news by aggressive FLUXUS art collectors Gilbert and Lila Silverman in Bloomfield Hills, Michigan.

On the same day, the U.S. House finally passes a Senate-passed civil-rights bill prohibiting racial discrimination in the sale or rental of about 80 percent of the nation's housing. Meanwhile, four-hundred to five-hundred Colgate University students and faculty members stage a sit-in at the main university administrative building to protest discriminatory fraternity housing practices.

It's reported that North Vietnamese troops and equipment are continuing to infiltrate South Vietnam on an unabated scale since the March 31 partial bombing halt called by President Johnson.

On April 11, a "Humphrey for President" campaign office opens in downtown Washington, D.C. It's conveniently located midway between Andy Ryan's home on 16th Street and his law office on DeSales.

This news doesn't generate nearly the interest that is created by Defense Secretary Clark Clifford's announcement that the Pentagon will call up 24,500 military reservists to be used in Vietnam. "But," says Clifford, "the administration does not intend to go beyond a ceiling of 549,500 troops!"

In an April 13 press release, Senator Robert Kennedy says that the United States must abandon the idea that "foreign commitments take precedence over the welfare of our own people." And U.S. Justice Department officials acknowledge that the methods of riot control following Martin Luther King's death were based on the minimum use of gunfire.

In response, Chicago Mayor Richard Daley instructs Chicago police to "shoot to kill" arsonists and to "shoot to maim or cripple" looters in future rioting.

Reacting strongly to Chicago Mayor Richard Daley's April 15 "shoot to kill" instruction, New York City Mayor John Lindsay says, "We happen to think that protection of life . . . is more important than protecting property."

A settlement is reached in the Memphis, Tennessee sanitation men's strike, the specific action that brought the Rev. Martin Luther King, Jr. to the city and to his death.

Israel agrees to a fact-finding United Nations mission to investigate the conditions of civilians in the Arab areas occupied by Israel if the mission also examines the Jewish communities living in Arab countries. On the same day, April 18, Israel expropriates twenty-nine acres of Palestinian land near the Wailing Wall in the Old City in Jerusalem.

While President Johnson briefs former President Dwight Eisenhower about recent developments in the Vietnam War, North Vietnam rejects all sites proposed by the United States for preliminary peace talks. Senator Robert Kennedy says that the United States should not quibble about the site for preliminary peace negotiations with North Vietnam.

United Nations Secretary General U Thant on April 20 expresses concern about the effects of Israel's scheduled military parade in Jerusalem on May 2. On the same day, British politician Enoch Powell says Britain should curtail the immigration of non-whites and encourage those already in Britain to leave the country.

The United States, Britain and the Soviet Union sign an agreement pledging international cooperation in the rescue of endangered astronauts. This is particularly important in light of the numerous space launches by Russia and the United States so far in 1968, including the April 22 launch of the Soviet Union's communications satellite Molniya-1. Space shots by Russia or the United States are averaging about one per week.

On the same day, the Overseas Press Club presents its prize for distinguished achievement in foreign journalism to Eric Pace for his writing on the 1967 Arab-Israeli war. And Trinity College students, in Hartford, Connecticut, hold their president captive in his office for three hours to force acceptance of an enlarged scholarship program for Negroes and academic courses on Afro-American culture and history.

On April 25 a Jordanian cabinet realignment ousts two ministers who opposed the operation of Arab guerrilla bands on Jordanian soil. And Israeli police break up an unauthorized demonstration by Arab women in East Jerusalem.

Algerian President Houri Boumedienne escapes serious injury as gunmen open fire on his limousine in Algiers.

Even Bermuda has civil strife when Negro youths break store windows and throw Molotov cocktails in the capital city of Hamilton during a two-day riot.

And, finally, Vice President Humphrey is heard from . . . when he states "there is no place in U.S. politics for the Stokely Carmichaels or white extremists." And not to be outdone, former Vice President Richard Nixon says that U.S. Negroes need "more black ownership, black pride and black power . . . in the constructive sense of that oft-misapplied term."

Former undersecretary of state George Ball replaces former labor attorney Arthur Goldberg, uncle of Chicago's Gerry Goldberg [Alec Ramsay's 4th floor hallmate in U of M's Michigan House dorm], as U.S. Ambassador to the United Nations. Goldberg vehemently denies there's a rift between himself and President Johnson.

Vice President Humphrey was polishing the biggest announcement of his life, which he intended to release on the morning of April 27. The nation's newspapers couldn't contain themselves when they learned that *"V.P. Hubert Horatio Humphrey formally announces his candidacy for the Democratic nomination for U.S. President."* On the same day, an estimated eighty-seven thousand demonstrators march against the Vietnam War in New York City, somewhat blunting the media impact of Humphrey's announcement.

Vice President Humphrey says that if elected U.S. president he "cannot promise *not* to send U.S. troops abroad" in case of Communist expansion.

On a non-political note, Senator Warren Magnuson's (D-Wash.) office announces the discovery of relics of the earliest known human being in the Americas, who probably lived eleven thousand to twelve thousand years ago. Magnuson is the senior U.S. senator from attorney Andy Ryan's home state.

As April ends, New York Governor Nelson Rockefeller enters the race for the Republican presidential nomination. Former Vice President Richard Nixon is counseled by Dwight Chapin and Ron Ziegler to welcome Rockefeller into the fray, and Nixon does so in a press release.

On May 1, 1968, Senator Robert Kennedy says that as the strongest nation in the world, the United States should not be concerned over whether it would "lose face" by agreeing to North Vietnamese proposals about a site for diplomatic talks.

In his first campaign trip after announcing his presidential candidacy, Vice President Humphrey on May 2 calls for "a new and complete national commitment to human rights."

As if on cue, caravans drawn by mules start from various parts of the country toward Washington, D.C., as the Poor People's Campaign begins. President Johnson says that federal officials have made "extensive preparations" for the Poor People's Campaign. Campaign leaders will not be discouraged.

Czechoslovak CP First Secretary Alexander Dubcek arrives in Moscow for talks about his country's current liberalization campaign. Two days later, on May 5, reports indicate major tensions between Soviet leaders and Dubcek during their talks in Moscow.

Student demonstrations spread to major provincial French universities on May 7. The same day finds Tunisia breaking ties with Syria. And Algeria announces that former Algerian army major Amar Mellah has been arrested and charged with being the principal instigator of the April 25 assassination attempt against President Houri Boumedienne.

And, of course, heavy fighting continues in Saigon.

In the Indiana Democratic presidential primary, Senator Robert Kennedy defeats Senator Eugene McCarthy with 42 percent of the vote against 27 percent. Both candidates applaud UAW delegates for re-electing Walter Reuther as UAW president.

The next day, May 8, UAW conventioneers greet Vice President Humphrey with a two-minute ovation. Clearly, he expects to receive endorsements from all major labor unions except possibly the Teamsters, who are still smarting over Bobby Kennedy's shoddy treatment of Jimmy Hoffa.

In Algeria, the national oil and gas combine, Sontrach, takes over fourteen foreign-owned oil and gas distribution companies. And an estimated one thousand Communist troops continue fighting in and around the Cholon district in Saigon. Concurrently, the U.S. State Department confirms that the North Koreans have shifted the captured U.S.S. *Pueblo* from Wonsan's harbor to another location.

West Germany and the United States again discuss the costs of maintaining American troops in West Germany.

On May 9, the UAW convention greets Senator Robert Kennedy with a forty-five second ovation. Vice President Humphrey smiles later when he has a chance to tell Elin Lindström: "I guess my one hundred and twenty second ovation, compared to RFK's forty-five second ovation, makes me the winner. Now, we just have to figure out the best way to maintain my momentum!"

The same day, a Poor People's Campaign caravan leaves Boston headed for Washington, D.C. Participants leave from Los Angeles the next day. Folks are traveling to Washington from every corner of America!

May 10 is a big day in Paris. North Vietnam and the United States begin peace talks in Paris. And an estimated thirty thousand students gather outside the Sorbonne in Paris, demanding the removal of police from university buildings.

To help facilitate the Poor People's Campaign march on Washington, the U.S. National Park Service issues a thirty-seven day renewable permit to allow the Poor People's Campaign to erect its plywood-and-canvas shantytown in Washington, D.C. The first marchers are expected to arrive May 11.

While other presidential candidates maintain low profiles, Senator Robert Kennedy continues to issue daily press releases. In his May 12 release, Kennedy proposes a minimum income tax to prevent certain wealthy individuals from escaping all taxation.

◄ Chapter 22 ►

*Instead of a Silly FLUXUS Birthday Performance,
Elin Delivers Shocking News to Horatio in
His Office Adjacent to the White House*

Monday, May 13, 1968

It's Monday afternoon, May 13, 1968, and Vice President Humphrey is in his spacious corner office in the Executive Office Building for a briefing with the lawyer and Democratic operative, Andrew Gallagher Ryan, Sr., Humphrey's executive aide Lawrence Gartner and three others.

"Before we get started on the campaign stuff," Gartner says, "has everyone seen the White House document from yesterday morning that confirms President Johnson and Clark Clifford are going to re-examine military needs in Vietnam? Evidently, they haven't yet decided whether more troops will be necessary."

Ryan chimes in, "And I trust we're all up to speed regarding the March 10th Gallup Poll that reports 49 percent of interviewees think the United States made a mistake by sending troops to fight in Vietnam."

Vice President Humphrey says, "Well, I'm far more concerned about Nixon's March 9th comment that he will not elaborate on his plans to end the Vietnam War because he's unwilling to reveal 'his bargaining positions in advance.' Frankly, I don't believe he has a plan. Nobody has a God-damned plan, and we need to tackle this matter immediately."

Humphrey continues, "And United Nations Secretary General U Thant hasn't helped President Johnson one whit with his call for an unconditional cessation of United States bombing in North Vietnam."

"So noted," Ryan declares rather dismissively. "Now, let's move on to the main reason we're here. This is how I see it. Despite what he said at the end of March about not seeking nor accepting the nomination, there's still an outside chance that LBJ will opt for another term. But, frankly, right now the odds in this town are probably running 80–20 against his trying for another term. And speaking from my perspective as his attorney—at least when it comes to the broadcast properties being held in trust for Lyndon and Lady Bird—I don't think he's gonna run!

"On the other hand, there's no question that Nixon will get the Republican's nod come the August convention in Miami."

Gartner pipes up, "Okay, here's what we now know about Nixon's current strategy. These creeps are going to concentrate on the seven battleground states on this map." Gartner is talking as he unfolds a small color-coded map and lays it on the table in front of the vice president.

An unsmiling third man named Elmer Archie pipes up with his two cents worth. "Mr. Vice President, the larger map over on the side table also highlights California, Illinois, Texas, Ohio, Pennsylvania, Michigan and New York . . . *plus* New Jersey, Wisconsin and Missouri. Each is a state where the Nixon Republicans think you'll be their main opposition. And, of course, there are the five peripheral southern states that George Wallace clearly owns. Together, these states have 298 electoral votes. Nixon needs to win at least 153 of them to combine with his almost certain 117 electoral votes from other states."

Ryan says, "Look, Mr. Vice President, you can see that Nixon's strategy of targeting the individual states contrasts sharply with his 1960 campaign against Kennedy. Remember, that's when

Nixon stupidly promised he would personally visit all fifty states.

"We all know it was that absurd, irrational commitment that caused Nixon to lose in 1960. Simply put, the candidate wasted far too much valuable time and resources in low-priority, low-return states."

Vice President Humphrey chimes in, "Well, maybe that's all true. But you can't discount old man Kennedy's money, plus all of their labor union connections."

"Except for the damn Teamsters, which Hoffa insists on keeping in the Republicans' camp," grumbles Archie.

Ryan ignores their interruptions and presses forward. "What I'm saying is that in 1960 Nixon simply wound up taking his eye off the ball in order to deliver on an irrelevant, unrealistic and totally unnecessary promise."

———

At this point, one of Vice President Humphrey's female staffers enters the office and quietly lays a folded note on the table in front of the vice president. Humphrey opens it and blinks twice as he glances at the simple, albeit sarcastically toned, handwritten message: "Miss Sweden is here." Evidently Elin was more than a casual visitor.

Humphrey gazes momentarily at the note, trying not to appear distracted. As usual, too many things are happening at one time. It's sometimes almost enough to scramble an old man's brain.

The vice president decides to abruptly end the meeting, and thanks Ryan and the others for coming by.

With a flourish of his hand, Humphrey dismisses them with, "Some really good stuff here, guys. Thanks for your fine efforts.

Let's keep moving forward. You all know what needs to be done next. There's nothing that can't wait until tomorrow morning's meeting, right?"

There was, of course, but all the guys could see that the vice president had, almost suddenly, become less focused. Gartner glances at his secret angel, Andrew Gallagher Ryan, and raises an eyebrow. Nobody in the room has the will to try continuing the conversation.

So, each man gathers up his own papers and slips them into briefcases. The maps are carefully folded and stowed, and the conferees bid each other adieu.

As they exit through the left side door of the vice president's office, another of Humphrey's assistants escorts Elin along the right hand aisle of the administrative bullpen.

As they approach a second door to the vice president's impressive corner office overlooking the West Wing of the White House, Elin sees Larry Gartner scurrying the other way down the parallel aisle. He's hoping she won't notice him, but Elin throws him a deceivingly cheerful and lilting, "Oh, good morning, Mr. Gartner."

Gartner ignores her greeting, a slight others more familiar with Elin might consider a tactical error. But Elin's troubled mind is focused like a laser on another matter. There's something in her life right now far more important than Horatio's sniveling, conniving weasel of an aide-de-camp. She is ushered into the vice president's inner sanctum, and the doors are closed.

The couple exchanges the kind of formal, stilted pleasantries that somehow seem appropriate in the nation's Executive Office Building. Except for a firm handshake, there's no physical contact between the two lovers.

But there's electricity in the air. Something's up, but Elin's Horatio can't quite put his finger on it. And then, in a flash, he thinks he knows what going on.

Silly as it may seem—at this moment and in this place—the vice president figures it's got to be one of Elin's patented "anytime" birthday gifts . . . a mini-FLUXUS performance which has endeared her to many friends who've enjoyed her impromptu, vest-pocket-sized celebrations. Except that his birthday still is almost two weeks away . . . on the 27th!

Elin's attractive, scrubbed, fresh face is twisted into a somewhat ironic smile as she says, "Horatio, I have a little surprise for you."

The vice president's face illuminates. "Ah-ha", he replies, "I thought so. A pleasant and welcome respite from the pressures and grind of helping to run the free world, is it?"

"Well, maybe not exactly," replies Elin in measured tones as she turns her head to check that both office doors are tightly shut.

She moves closer to Humphrey's side of the desk, and surprises him by taking his right hand in hers. And then she places both of their hands, ever so gently, on her stomach. The vice president tries to draw his hand away. "Maybe this isn't exactly the place. . . . "

But Elin persists. Sweetly and deliberately, she smiles and sighs, "Horatio, you and me . . . we're going to have a baby!"

The vice president's hands drop limply to his sides as he stands up. With his mouth hanging open, he tries to fathom her words. They seem real and unreal at the same time. As she sees the blood draining from the vice president's face, Elin implores her friend, "Horatio, please tell me you're as happy as I am. Please do that for us."

Humphrey is obviously taken aback. He's mentally distressed and visibly shaken. His face turns visibly ashen as he pleads, "Oh my Lord, no! This is a joke, isn't it? It's not at all funny. Tell me it's not so."

He babbles on, "You're playing a very unfunny joke on me, right? It can't be true. I mean, it's not possible. We, aaahh . . . I always use protection. I mean, you know that. But of course you do. For God's sakes, Elin, you were there!"

"Yes, my dear, I was there," she replies quietly.

The vice president's mind isn't working like he wants it to. After a short pause, he exclaims, almost in terror, "You're really not joking with me, are you?"

He starts again, "Now look here, Elin, we've got to remain calm and view this matter realistically. For starters, you do realize, don't you, that this is the year 1968. It's an election year, and I intend to be elected president this November."

And then, in an icy, matter-of-fact tone she has never heard from him before, the vice president says, "You'll just have to get an abortion, Elin. I can arrange it right here in Washington. It's simple, quick, safe and won't cost you anything." She wonders if he's said these same words to others.

"We can't take any chances on messing things up. There's simply too much at stake. Too many people are depending on me. Too much money is already contributed. Too many promises made. I can be ruined. You can appreciate that, I'm sure."

Elin turns away, weeping. It's the first time, ever, that Horatio can recall seeing Elin cry. Not even at her papa's funeral in Stockholm!

For the vice president, the situation before them is a no-brainer. He knows precisely what must be done to preserve his presidential aspirations.

For Elin, too, it's a no-brainer. After all, her hidden tape recorder has picked up the entire exchange.

As she slowly walks toward the door, Elin turns and

matter-of-factly says to the vice president of the United States,
"Oh, dear, I almost forgot. Happy Birthday, Horatio!"

Has she, or has she not, just delivered a FLUXUS birthday
greeting?

◄ Chapter 23 ►

The Vice President Meets the Lethal Dr. Moser in Andy Ryan's Home

TUESDAY, MAY 14, 1968

It's early afternoon and Andrew Gallagher Ryan, Sr., greets America's vice president at the front door. "Good afternoon, Mr. Vice President. Thanks so much for stopping by. You've met Dr. Moser before, I believe." Two Secret Service agents remain in the hallway.

"Peter and I have just been talking about how a single decision, good or bad, can reverberate for generations, and can even wind up affecting millions of people around the globe.

"For example," Ryan elaborates, "I remember when Franklin Roosevelt promised Saudi Arabia's King Ibn Saud that America would consult with the Arabs before deciding the future of Palestine. Unfortunately, Roosevelt died a few months after his meeting with Saud.

"And when Roosevelt's successor, Harry Truman, was asked to renew the American commitment to consult with the Arabs before the United Nations General Assembly in 1947, Truman replied, 'I'm sorry, gentlemen, but I have to account to the hundreds of thousands of constituents in America who are anxious for the success of Zionism. I do not have hundreds of thousands of Arabs or Moslems among my constituents!'"

"And because of President Truman's change in direction, on May 14, 1948, the Jewish state of Israel was born, and Palestine ceased to exist. The United States and other civilized countries have been paying a great price ever since for Truman's selfish political posturing.

"And the situation's going to worsen if the Republicans win in 1968, because super-rich American Zionists like Max Fisher and that fellow Taubman have lobbied hard on behalf of Israel. They and other American Zionists are in the habit of buying the votes of many Republicans in Congress, plus a fair number of maverick Democrats.

"Here's the bottom line, my friends: these guys and others are contributing millions of dollars every year—they call it *investing in their future*—so they can own thirty or forty core congressional Republicans. Guys like Fisher figure if they finance enough American political campaigns, they can have a chance of someday owning Congress and maybe even an American president. Do whatever it takes to cordon off and bury the Palestinians!

"I know for a fact that Fisher has already told business associates in Detroit that his oldest daughter, Mary, is assured of a White House job if Nixon becomes president. It just takes a lot of dough-re-mi. But most of all, dough!"

Ryan continues, "And even closer to home, I can tell you all about what's going on in my own family's homeland, Ireland. It's not a pretty picture. And the killing will get worse if the British don't modify their intransigent position on the human-rights issues."

Then, finally moving into the real reason for their three-way meeting, Ryan says, "Now Hubert, as you know, Dr. Moser here has been a loyal and significant contributor to our Democratic campaigns. He can be trusted implicitly to quietly manage in a most professional manner the little predicament you mentioned to me last night."

Ryan explains, "Arrangements have been made for Miss

Lindström to have an abortion tomorrow afternoon." He tells the vice president that he must speak with her as soon as possible today. "And make sure you use a secure line, Hubert. And no taping!"

Not in a mood to be scolded by Ryan or anybody else, but clearly unable to duck the issue, the vice president replies, "Of course. I'll instruct her to fly into National. However, I know she'll probably insist on driving down to D.C. She loves to drive, you know."

"Well, that'll be fine," says Ryan, "just so she reaches Dr. Moser's office between two and three in the afternoon. Peter's a busy man, and he's doing us a big favor by squeezing the girl into his schedule on short notice."

"By the way, Hubert," Ryan asks, trying hard to seem nonchalant, "I wonder what kind of car the young lady drives?"

Humphrey, not realizing the consequences riding on his answer, quickly responds, "Why, I've heard she drives a new red Chevy Camaro convertible with a white top."

Appearing to not even hear the answer to his own question, Ryan says, "Okay, look here, the sooner we get this bit of unpleasantness behind us, the better. And it's imperative that only the three of us, plus Miss What's-Her-Name, ever know about this little matter. Understood? Do we agree?"

Humphrey nods, and says, "If you gentlemen will excuse me for a moment, nature calls. Be right back." The vice president walks, seemingly with some difficulty, down the generous five-foot wide hallway toward Ryan's guest bathroom.

With Humphrey gone from the drawing room, Ryan steps closer to Dr. Moser and in a low voice coolly tells him to kill Elin. "We can't take any chances, Peter. You know what to do, and then how to dispose of the body. Just like the last time we had a problem."

Then, in a practiced theatrical voice loud enough for Humphrey to overhear in the bathroom, Ryan dismisses Dr. Moser with, "Thanks so much for stopping by, Peter. I'm sure everything will be just fine. I know you're busy and I'll give Hubert your regards. And please tell Mrs. Moser hello from Delphine and me."

Ryan adds, in a hushed, no-nonsense tone, "And one more thing Peter, be sure to call me tomorrow night at home."

◄ **C h a p t e r   2 4** ►

Startled by Elin's Unexpected News,
Alec Drops His Cookies on Her New White Carpet

Tuesday, May 14, 1968

Alec Ramsay is in Elin's small but clean and well-organized kitchen pouring himself a glass of fresh goat's milk. He picks three chocolate Oreos out of a large Orefors cut-crystal bowl— one that Elin's papa had given her momma on the first anniversary of their loving marriage—and strolls toward the sitting room that faces north, four floors above Manhattan's East 60th Street.

Elin starts speaking even before Alec enters the room. "I'm driving down to Washington tomorrow for an abortion," she says matter-of-factly. Ramsay drops his cookies on Elin's new white carpet, but manages not to spill any of the goat's milk.

She puts an index finger to her lips before he can say, "You're doing *what* tomorrow?"

They argue politely at first, and then more vociferously, about the merits of her risking an abortion. "Look," says Ramsay heatedly, "this is a stupid conversation."

Elin's pragmatism startles Ramsay. "Don't get testy with me, Buster. Figure it out. I'm unmarried and I intend to remain so for a long, long time because there's lots I need to do before settling down with a family.

"Besides, Horatio wants the abortion, too!" Oh, oh! She's spilled the beans!

Ramsay pauses momentarily, for he's not heard about this

Horatio character before. *Jesus Christ*, Ramsay thinks to himself, *this guy must be a first-class jerk. Besides, what kind of real man would call himself Horatio?*

He's probably one of Elin's Manhattan street performance friends, Ramsay muses to himself. *What a performance he must have put on for her. Naw, maybe not, 'cause aren't all those street guys queer?*

Or maybe, he figures, *she got knocked up by somebody working for Pan Am or at the Swedish Embassy in Washington. After all*, Ramsay again murmurs to himself, *who wouldn't want to have a baby that shares Elin's gene pool? I mean, really!*

Then, almost absentmindedly, Ramsay blurts out, "Who the hell ever heard of a Swede named Horatio?" Startled by his outburst, Elin can only imagine what's going through Ramsay's mind at this moment.

Ramsay calms down and turns back toward Elin. "Look, Doll, if you're absolutely determined to go through with this nonsense, then at least you've got to let me drive you down to D.C. Just look at yourself. You're in no condition to walk, much less drive anywhere by yourself."

Elin glares at Ramsay. "Absolutely not! I'm fine now, and I'll be just fine tomorrow," she snaps.

Once again, Ramsay thinks to himself, *Whoa, here she goes blowing me off again.* In his mind, Elin is once again rejecting his attempt at kindness. The last time, he recalls, she didn't want him in Stockholm for her papa's funeral.

Christ, maybe she wouldn't be in this pickle if I had been persistent enough, and gone to Sweden with her. Naaahh, he finally admits to himself, *that's just my latest "rationalization-of-convenience."* Ramsay knows that he doesn't have a clue as to what is really going on.

Already used to Elin's independent nature, Alec is convinced she can't be dissuaded from driving to Washington the next day.

But that doesn't make Ramsay any more pleased about what he considers to be Elin's selfish and foolish decision regarding her baby.

With his ruddy face turning an even deeper red, Ramsay's simmering irritation suddenly turns to anger and he stalks toward the front door of Elin's apartment.

Elin's apartment door slams shut behind Ramsay as he exits without another word. There's not even a parting glance toward the woman he loves.

Elin breaks into a shivering fit of tears. With Alexander gone, there's no one left she can lean on or trust. It's all so sad. Truly heartbreaking!

◂ C h a p t e r 2 5 ▸

A Mystery Unfolds in the Dank,
Dimly Lighted Parking Garage Beneath
Elin's Apartment at 220 East 60th

WEDNESDAY, MAY 15, 1968

Two well-dressed individuals, a gentleman and a lady, walk quickly toward the two elevators servicing the basement garage of Elin's building. Each carries a large tote bag. The woman presses the "UP" button, and a door opens immediately. They step aboard and press "4."

Moments later the other elevator door opens at the garage level, and Elin steps out. She's carrying her blue, medium-sized Samsonite hard-shell bag and a small camera case which she locks in the car trunk.

Elin doesn't notice a small radio transmitter that's stuck magnetically to the passenger side of her car, just above the rear bumper.

As Elin lowers the automatic white fabric top on her convertible, her car's beefy 350-liter small-block V-8 roars to life with a throaty resonance that seems even more muscular because of the sound waves bouncing off the concrete ceiling and walls.

Because she has backed into her reserved parking space, like she knows policemen, FBI agents and other authority figures are trained to do, it's easy for Elin to pull forward out of her space and move quickly up the ramp before turning west onto East 60th. She moves past Yellowfinger's on the southeast corner of Third and East 60th, and then past Bloomingdale's which takes up the entire next block between Third and Lexington.

The light at Lexington turns red, and she stops in the midst of perhaps two dozen Yellow cabs. What they say about Manhattan traffic is never truer than during morning and afternoon rush-hours.

A dark-colored nondescript sedan, which has been illegally parked at the curb in front of All Saints' Episcopal Church, next to Elin's apartment building, noses its way into the traffic flow half a block behind Elin. Even if she had noticed the mysterious car, Elin would have ignored it because her mind is crammed with many more important thoughts and emotions.

As the light at Lexington Avenue flashes green for Elin, another convertible—this one white, with its dark blue top still up—is easing up the ramp of Elin's apartment building and onto East 60th. Already, it's at least a block and a half behind Elin. And the heavy morning traffic will make it almost impossible for the white convertible to gain on her.

It's imperative that Alec Ramsay's gleaming white Pontiac faux-GTO, with its blue ragtop, bold hood-scoops and distinctive dual dark blue stripes painted on the bonnet, is able to spot Elin's car before it's too late.

Hemmed in by the oppressively slow morning rush-hour traffic, Ramsay reflects upon the mysterious telephone call to his apartment last night from the stranger with a curiously high-pitched voice who said she lived near Washington, D.C.

The woman had identified herself as a doctor's receptionist who'd overheard a conversation in late afternoon that seemed to indicate a female acquaintance of Ramsay's named Elaine, or maybe Erin, was in for some serious trouble in Washington. No specifics, but just enough sketchy info for Ramsay to conclude that Elin was truly in some sort of real danger.

When he pressed the caller for more details—like why did the caller know to call *him*, and how had she obtained his name and phone number—the informant hesitated for a moment and then said in her peculiar, high-pitched voice, "Not now, Marian! Peter needs some coffee and I've got to put the kids to bed." Then the phone connection went dead! Not surprisingly, Alec couldn't recall ever having been called by a woman's name.

For Ramsay, the mystery centered on the "why" rather than on the "how." After all, any fool can find his name, address and phone number in the 1968 Manhattan telephone book. On the other hand, he knows there's also an Alec Ramsey—last name spelled with an "e" as the second vowel instead of an "a"—living at River House along the East River in the mid-fifties. He's a theatrical producer married to a Broadway musical actress. "Real nice man, too, that Ramsey," Ramsay has been assured by mutual acquaintances.

In fact, Manhattan Bell's information operators often confuse the two Alecs in the same way they mix up the two Carroll Carrolls who live in midtown. One Carroll Carroll works with Alec Ramsay at J. Walter Thompson Company, while the other Carroll Carroll is an executive at *The New York Times*.

Curiously, JWT's Mr. Carroll knows rather well both the show-business entrepreneur Alec Ramsey and JWT's Alec Ramsay. But then it seems that JWT's Carroll knows practically everybody in Manhattan, from *Daily Variety's* editor, Abel Green, to Dan Seymour, the former radio-soap-opera-announcer-turned-President/CEO at JWT.

◄ Chapter 26 ►

Tracking Elin's Red Camaro Convertible in Early-Morning Rush-Hour Traffic

WEDNESDAY, MAY 15, 1968

Very early this morning—in fact, just shortly after Johnny Carson had signed off of his late night show on NBC, the Peacock Network—Alec Ramsay silently wandered down the back stairs into the parking garage underneath 220 East 60th. Although his heart was racing, Ramsay tried hard to appear calm and composed.

In fact, his mind was agitated and still muddled by the strange telephone call he had received a short while before. Ramsay's body was sweaty and trembling—despite the year-round chill of the underground garage—at the thought of how easy it had been for an out-of-nowhere stranger to obtain information about him. But it could turn out to be a blessing if the caller's information some-how helped him protect Elin.

Ramsay knew he would have to be clever and stealthy because of the three large black security video cameras mounted from the ten-foot-high garage ceiling. He didn't know whether the cameras were real or fake, or if the doorman Spagna or anybody else ever checked them out.

Certainly Spagna never mentioned monitoring cameras as part of his job description, on the rather frequent occasions when he would recite his job description while bitching about being paid less than some doormen who worked in nearby but less prestigious buildings. Ramsay figured it was merely another of Spagna's crude ploys to boost his income from tips by sympathetic residents.

Ramsay stopped momentarily near the rear of Elin's Camaro, and then made a slight move with his torso so that he appeared to be bending over to look more closely at something on the car's trunk door. He could have been examining a stone chip, or maybe a white spot of poop where a seagull, Canada goose or black crow had scored a direct hit. But the reason really didn't matter.

As he studied the imaginary "something" on Elin's car, Ramsay bent his knees slightly and leaned over just far enough to reach down with his right hand to affix a magnetic electronic homing device near the rear bumper. It was a curious-looking two-part device that Ramsay came across in a vacant classroom one evening during his Signal Corps training at Fort Monmouth. It had fit nicely into his large khaki-colored duffel bag, which in turn had fit nicely into the trunk of his car of the moment, a dark green 1951 Chevrolet two-door sedan with the green-and-white-checkered terry-cloth slipcovers held in place with wide elastic bands.

If Ramsay's instinct and suspicions were correct, then maybe the device could help him keep tabs on his lady friend as she drove south toward Washington for a mid-afternoon rendezvous with Vice President Humphrey's abortion doctor. Having "lost" Elin's position in Manhattan's byzantine morning traffic, possibly due to interference from all the tall buildings, Ramsay guesses she'll take the Lincoln Tunnel under the Hudson River, which will feed her directly onto the New Jersey Turnpike and then south.

A few minutes after exiting the tunnel Ramsay can "see" Elin's car by listening to beeps on the audiometer-type device taped to his dashboard. Despite a weak signal, he can tell she's headed south at what seems to be normal speed. But that strikes Ramsay as a little peculiar inasmuch as traffic on the turnpike going south from the city is flowing well, and because "normal speed" for

Elin's Camaro normally is a few clicks faster than everyone else on the road.

Several state troopers, in fact, had in the past attested to Elin's "lead foot" since late 1967 when she acquired her hot "red flash." But Elin always seemed prepared for the worse. So, when confronted by the police, Elin smiled brightly and simply whipped out of her purse an official-looking document from the Swedish Embassy requesting that special consideration please be given to the bearer. Thus, she had yet to receive her first traffic citation!

Ramsay still couldn't help but wonder about Elin's relatively slow speed. Can something be wrong with her car? Is Elin feeling okay? Certainly she wouldn't be trying to conserve gasoline. Especially today!

Before long, Ramsay thinks he's spotted Elin's car far ahead. Accelerating so as to close the gap between them, the amateur sleuth picks up binoculars lying next to him on the passenger seat. Steering with his knees, Ramsay uses both hands in an effort to focus the binocs on Elin's car.

As he draws a bead on the red Camaro convertible, which is gleaming in the sunlight and looks particularly sweet with its top down, Ramsay can't help but notice a nondescript grey car not far behind Elin. It has two figures in the front seat and is driving in the right hand lane. Ramsay wonders why the grey car is driving so slowly behind Elin when it can easily pass her.

Drawing closer and keeping his focus on the grey car for a moment, Ramsay is startled to see through the back window that the passenger is gripping something in his left hand that looks like a handgun. With his mind on overload trying to process information—last night's mystery phone call, a guy holding a gun, the grey car's slower-than-normal speed—Ramsay realizes that Elin's right hand turn signal is flashing. He prays she isn't planning to pull off now and stop on the berm. Certainly not here. Not now!

Ramsay is relieved as he watches Elin continue on for another half mile to the long sweeping exit leading into a Texaco service plaza. *Bingo, that's it*, Ramsay thinks to himself. He figures that Elin has been driving slower than usual because she needed to conserve petrol until she can reach a gas station. That's the good news!

The bad news? Ramsay watches as the grey Plymouth sedan trails Elin into the Texaco station, and slowly pulls up to a gas pump immediately to the right of Elin's convertible. Ramsay closes in on the scene, trying to remain inconspicuous—a silly notion under the circumstances, considering his car was anything but inconspicuous!

He assiduously avoids Elin's direct line of sight, for he certainly doesn't want to alarm nor upset her. How terrible if she were to think he's following her, especially when she had specifically and aggressively told him just yesterday to "butt out!"

"Hardly an intelligent way to nurture a healthy, trusting, long-term relationship. Just stupid!," Alec Ramsay mumbles to himself.

◄ Chapter 27 ►

Death by Explosion at a Texaco Station
Along the New Jersey Turnpike

WEDNESDAY, MAY 15, 1968

The upbeat music and vocals of an obscure Swedish group called the Hootenanny Singers play loudly on Elin's Delco eight-track system, almost drowning out her voice as she yells to the Texaco attendant, "Please fill it up with high-test."

One can only guess about the kaleidoscope of thoughts thrashing around in Elin's head as many gallons of high-octane gasoline are force-fed into her car by a squinty-eyed thirty-something "man who wears the star." He looks nothing like any of the four guys who used to sing Texaco's theme song weekly on Milton Berle's *Texaco Star Theatre* television comedy show.

Elin is oblivious to the grey sedan that's sitting at the pump to her right. Indeed, she would be flabbergasted to know there's a black-and-white photograph of her on the front bench seat between the two men. It's a recent picture, too, taken by the scar-faced man who had been lurking across the street from her apartment building with a telephoto lens-equipped camera.

Moreover, there's no way Elin can know about the hand gun that's already cocked and about to be leveled at her head.

With an engaging smile and a West Virginia twang, the Texaco attendant asks his good-lookin' customer if he can please check her fluids. Completely missing the attempt at humor, Elin replies pleasantly enough, "Not today, thank you. I'm really in a bit of a hurry." She hands the fellow a crisp fifty-dollar bill, and he trots toward the station to get change after motioning to the grey car that he'll be right back.

As soon as the attendant starts walking away, Alec Ramsay coolly strolls over to the gas pump next to the grey car. He deftly withdraws the wide-mouth nozzle attached to the long flexible black hose, takes careful aim, and launches a powerful stream of gasoline through the open window, drenching both occupants. The startled passenger's 45-mm pistol drops onto the floor. Both men are stunned, and begin jabbering loudly at him in some sort of guttural language.

Elin, somewhat lost in reverie, finally senses the nearby commotion and jerks her face to the right. She's dumbfounded and momentarily confused by the tableau unfolding right next to her.

Elin thinks she sees Alec Ramsay, but knows she must be dreaming. She's totally shaken out of her lethargy when Ramsay starts shouting at her over the music and surrounding din.

"Get outta here, Elin. Now! Forget about your damned money! No questions. I'll explain later. I love you madly, Doll. GO, GO, GO!!!"

In this superheated moment, Elin has heard nothing. Instinctively, though, she turns the ignition switch just as the gas-soaked passenger in the car next to her retrieves his pistol from the floor. The man, his eyes partially blinded by gasoline and with a deep scar running diagonally across his face, aims the pistol past the head of his dazed driver-partner who is writhing furiously as he struggles to open the locked driver's side car door.

An instant before the stranger squeezes the trigger, Ramsay tosses his lighted Zippo six feet through the open passenger side window of the grey Plymouth.

Ka-boom! **Ka-boom!!!**

Elin hears two explosions; one is the deafening report of a 45-mm pistol. Another is the muffled roar of exploding gasoline. The second *ka-boom* nearly tears the roof off of the grey Plymouth and almost instantly incinerates both occupants.

It's superfluous that the bullet meant for Elin had struck the other driver's head and splattered pieces of his skull and brain matter on the pavement in a colorful, mosaic pattern. Undoubtedly some of Elin's friends in Manhattan and Wiesbaden would have considered the scene to be an especially artful FLUXUS project. *Ultimate* performance art, perhaps?

In that same instant, Elin floors her accelerator and rockets toward the exit ramp from the Texaco station back onto the southbound turnpike.

Ramsay picks himself up off the ground, where he was thrown by the explosive concussion, and races toward his white car with the dark blue stripes on the bonnet and trunk. He turns and sees the attendant dashing out the door with Elin's change. Alec wonders if the attendant is merely stunned, hopelessly stupid, or both.

Through the heat and sound of the raging fire, Ramsay shouts the words, "I'm going for help," knowing it doesn't really matter whether or not the attendant sees or hears him. Alec jumps into his idling GTO, slams it into first gear and almost loses control as he spins the steering wheel hard-left and speeds away.

The baffled attendant, still holding Elin's change in his right hand, runs over to the nearby pump island and picks up the water hose used for topping off car radiators and swabbing minor fuel spills. He frantically turns on the spigot, and jams his right thumb into the end of the hose so that it'll pee a stream of water he knows will be no match for the conflagration raging in front of him.

Having already consumed one grey Plymouth and two corpses,

the fire now threatens to destroy the entire pump island and its equipment.

Once safely on the turnpike headed south, Ramsay makes an illegal "u-ey" across the median grass and heads back north toward the Lincoln Tunnel and Manhattan. Whew, no highway patrol car in sight. Yet!

———

After re-parking his car in the garage underneath 220 East 60th, Ramsay grabs his briefcase from behind the front seat and heads on foot toward J. Walter Thompson's office at 420 Lex. After a brisker walk than usual, he arrives at the office only a few minutes later than his usual starting time. More literally than he may have wished, another of Alec Ramsay's workdays has started off with a real bang!

———

Back at the fire-ravaged Texaco station, the hapless white-trash-bred Texaco attendant is speaking almost incoherently to three New Jersey state troopers and a local municipal fire inspector. "Like ah told 'ja, I was inside a-gittin change fo da gal when it happened. Po thing, so scared she gone off without her money."

The lead trooper insists upon taking possession of the new fifty-spot Elin had given the attendant. One trooper explains, "It's got fingerprints we'll need," as he starts to write out a receipt to cover the evidence. He then changes his mind and says, "Naw, you don't need a receipt. We're New Jersey state troopers, so you know you can trust us."

The attendant is terrified at the near-term prospect of having to break the news to Texaco's regional manager. He's unsure which to mention first . . . the fifty-dollar bill confiscated by the state policemen, or the fifty-thousand-plus that Texaco's insurance company will need to cough up for repairing the fire damage.

"Oh, yeah," the attendant guy yells as the troopers walk toward their patrol cars. "Thar was also this dude in, I think it was a white Pontiac. He did seen what happened. Said he was a-goin' to call you guys. He should be back anytime!"

The troopers look at each other, and shrug "yeah, fat chance." About the same odds, they agreed, as the poor sucker of a gas station attendant ever seeing his fifty-spot again!

◄ Chapter 28 ►

Checking Into, and Then Escaping From,
Dr. Moser's Clinic in Southwest Washington, D.C.

WEDNESDAY, MAY 15, 1968

Dr. Peter Moser's medical clinic is located in what appears to be a relatively new but plain-looking one-story building on Washington's seedy southwest side, but within sight of the U.S. Capitol.

The only identification on the building's front is a street number and the word "CLINIC" in ten-inch block letters formed from brushed aluminum. There's no mailbox, nor even a slot in the door, because the mail gets delivered to a box at the nearby postal substation. After all, why unnecessarily tempt the neighborhood kids, night people and other riff-raff who think it's cute or convenient to dispose of their garbage and used condoms in surprising places?

It's nearly three o'clock in the afternoon when Elin pulls up in front of the clinic, checks the address and then drives around a corner so she can park on the side street.

Having gone to school at Georgetown University, only three miles or so up Pennsylvania Avenue past the White House, Elin still knows her way around this part of town. She considers herself to be street smart and is reasonably comfortable here despite the area's reputation as a dangerous place to be, particularly after dusk.

Before getting out of the car, Elin jams her purse under the front seat. She deliberately stares at the key in her hand—and actually says the word "key" out loud—and then locks the Camaro from outside. Her Samsonite and camera bags are safely tucked away in the trunk. She knows one should never leave anything in sight, especially in this southwest D.C. neighborhood!

As Elin walks slowly toward the clinic, all she has are car keys and the clothes on her back.

She steps up to the metal front door—which is graced on both sides with narrow vertical Plexiglas windows protected by iron bars—and presses the brass-colored buzzer button. A moment later another buzzer sounds, and Elin pushes open the heavy steel door.

Once inside, she's greeted by a dour-looking middle-aged white woman who is seated behind a piece of thick plate glass.

Inexplicably, a flashback is triggered in Elin's mind: If this woman hadn't been clothed in white, Elin imagines it could have been the same broken-down, baggy-eyed lady she remembers selling movie tickets from inside the glass-enclosed box-office at the old Sherman Oaks Theater in the 15000 block of Ventura Boulevard in California's San Fernando Valley. Indeed, a friend once told Elin that it's the same theatre where William Inge's movie *Picnic* played for a record-setting several months in a row back in the late 1950s.

Elin—wondering what on earth triggered her flashback—is smart enough to realize that right now many dissonant thoughts are bouncing around her brain. She must be careful not to over-react.

The woman quickly escorts Elin through a door and hands her off to a nurse named Mabel, a large pock-faced woman with bad teeth and bad breath. Noting Mabel's aversion to smiling and her obvious poor self-image, Elin thinks to herself, *Well, these ladies fit right into the neighborhood!*

Figuring that Mabel is probably a jumbo-sized dyke, Elin envisions her playing linebacker on Sunday afternoons for the Redskins. *A real load, this one!*

Elin is ushered into a medium-sized procedures room equipped with the usual stirrups and a few other intriguing implements. The room is decorated in pretty pastels which seem to be enhanced by lots of natural light streaming in through the large chain-operated skylight above. The nurse asks Elin to repeat her name again, and then to spell it. "We can't be too careful now, can we, Dearie?"

"The Load" then brusquely instructs Elin to disrobe and to put on the standard-issue white cotton medical gown she's holding. It's a garment with no back and only two strings tied together to keep it from falling off Elin's shoulders and into a clump around her ankles!

Elin politely excuses herself and walks down the corridor to a bathroom so she can relieve herself one last time before exposing everything to Dr. Moser and his bag of specialty tools. She locks the door and sits down, reflecting one last time upon her decision and the procedure she's about to undergo.

Having already run the pros and cons through her mind a dozen or more times, Elin knows she has made the correct decision. *Or was it Horatio's decision?* At this point, does it really matter?

In her nearly naked solitude, Elin hears muffled voices, and is barely able to make out a conversation that's reverberating through the metal ductwork. For just a moment, she feels like an intruder listening in on somebody's private conversation. But as a woman with more than a passing familiarity with G2 techniques, this isn't the first time Elin has overheard somebody's private conversation.

Suddenly, Elin's body stiffens and involuntarily bolts upright as she hears one of the unknown voices speak her name, "Not sure how you say it, but it's spelled L-i-n-d-s-t-r-ö-m. Don't know if it means anything, but there are two dots on top of the 'o'."

Good God, the invisible voices are talking about her! The words that follow are chilling, and change Elin's innocent curiosity into downright fear. She can't even wait to squeeze or wipe the last drops of pee before jumping up, adjusting her backless gown and dashing back to the procedures room.

Elin notices immediately that the clothing she had left neatly folded in a pile has been moved. In fact, it's gone! Every stitch! Her clothing is nowhere in the room! When she asks the linebacker of a nurse where her stuff is, Mabel hesitates and then replies in her husky baritone, "Well, Dearie, Dr. Moser must have moved your clothes into his office." She adds cryptically, "Maybe he thinks you won't need them right away."

Fear grips Elin even tighter. When she instinctively moves toward the now-closed procedures-room door, the nurse blocks her way, and then excitedly shouts Dr. Moser's name through the closed door.

When Elin says, "Will you excuse me, please," and tries one more time to exit, Mabel the Linebacker grabs at her patient . . . and in so doing pulls off Elin's gown. Elin responds instantly by cold-cocking the uncooperative and unsympathetic nurse with a single chop to the throat.

The nurse collapses like dead weight right in front of the closed door. Elin turns the door lock from the inside and then jams a chair under the handle. The bottom rung of the chair rests firmly against Mabel's fat throat. Elin sits down on the chair with all her weight, and looks satisfied when she hears a rush of air expelled from her victim's mouth, together with a trace of blood.

Elin tries to pull on what remains of her badly ripped gown. She knows it's a hopeless task. Suddenly she vaults onto a grey metal cabinet and stretches her body to reach the lightweight chain drive that manually controls the skylight's mechanism.

Once the window is open, Elin pulls herself up and out of the skylight. Barefooted, she runs along the roof, shinnies down a large but flimsy aluminum downspout and dashes through the back alley toward her car. She's careful to avoid stepping on the broken wine bottles, needles and used condoms.

The afternoon's pre-rush-hour crowd hardly notices Elin. After all, this is the southwest side of America's capital city; a place where *strange* is as commonplace as in the Capitol Building itself.

By now, Dr. Moser has broken into the procedures room, which has been strangely silent since Mabel had shouted his name only moments earlier. He's appalled to find his nurse face-upward on the floor, possibly dead, and today's prize patient gone. Glancing upward, he realizes that things probably will be getting worse before better. Much worse!

The good doctor, realizing he is powerless over the situation and can do nothing except curse repeatedly to himself, reaches for a telephone. This is the one telephone call he absolutely doesn't want to make. But he has no choice. "Hello. Let me speak to Mr. Ryan," he orders with controlled anger and fear. "And make it quick. Tell him the doctor's calling."

———

Meantime, Elin has reached her car and located the back-up set of keys she had hidden months earlier inside the special magnetic key holder stuck inside the left rear wheel well. It was cheap insurance that she thought she might need someday. And it's paying off for her now, in spades! Who knew!?

Horatio's 1968 red Camaro RS/SS convertible starts immediately. With the roar of raw power, Elin feels a new surge of energy, excitement and purpose coursing through her mind and body. She moves carefully into the traffic flow, only now starting to understand that her life somehow has mercifully been spared. At least for now.

She's happy and fearful at the same time. But what she doesn't yet realize is that it was *quick-wittedness*—first, Alec Ramsay's action a few hours before, and now her own—that has twice saved her life on this day.

Still stark-naked under the thin and torn medical gown, Elin heads out Pennsylvania Avenue and then into Georgetown, toward the Swedish ambassador's house.

◄ Chapter 29 ►

Elin Seeks a Safe Haven at
Ambassador Wallenberg's Residence in Georgetown

WEDNESDAY, MAY 15, 1968

A bright red Camaro convertible slowly edges its way along Georgetown's Nebraska Avenue and turns in at the guardhouse in front of the legendary Swedish Embassy's Ambassadorial Residence at number 3900. Elin Lindström—looking a little strange partially swathed in a white cotton gown—speaks in Swedish to one of the two uniformed security staffers on duty.

Realizing that neither guard understands Swedish very well, she switches to English and asks for her friend and Ambassadorial Assistant Gunilla Nordström. After the customary call to the "big house," one of the security men signals "thumbs-up" to Elin.

Thus cleared for entry by the wave of a hand, Elin carefully drives up the winding and tree-lined driveway to the dark red brick Georgian-style main house built in 1924. Mrs. Nordström greets Elin warmly at the top of the hill while trying to ignore her skimpy attire.

After a brief conversation, Mrs. Nordström suggests that Elin drive around back to the large five-car garage that connects to the house via an enclosed two-story breezeway. Then, if Elin will wait a few minutes, she'll find a selection of clothes laid out on the bonnet of a long, shiny, black Cadillac sedan.

———

After exchanging her shredded white patient's gown for a beige skirt, cream-colored cashmere sweater and brown penny loafers, Elin walks into the mansion's kitchen through the connecting door. She's greeted once again by Mrs. Nordström, who had known both of Elin's parents since her days back in Eskilstuna, when Lars Lindström was editor of one of the two local newspapers.

Although it's obvious to Mrs. Nordström that Elin has been through some sort of harrowing experience, she decides against asking questions just now. There'll be time for that later!

Elin is shown to a third-floor bedroom suite, which has a full bath and a shower attached. The layout of the space reminds Elin, for some incongruent and possibly warped reason, of Kurt-Visby Rädisson's boat that night in Stockholm's harbor. Maybe it's the spaciousness of the room combined with the warm woods, carved white ceiling and wide mouldings, plus a large connecting bathroom with many luxurious pastel-colored towels stacked on a shelf.

Right now, however, nothing seems more pleasurable and reassuring to Elin than the prospect of simply soaking her entire body in a deep, warm bath. There's a separate shower to rinse her body and wash her medium-length blond hair. It's heaven, simply heaven. Elin says to herself, "What a difference an hour and a few miles can make!"

After toweling off and combing the snags out of her hair, Elin decides to phone Alec Ramsay in Manhattan. She really hopes he's at home.

Without even a "hello," she blurts out, "For the first time in my life, Alec, I was absolutely terrified this afternoon!"

Ramsay interrupts, "My God, Doll, where are you? Are you okay?"

"I'm in Georgetown, at the ambassador's home, and I'm fine."

"Well," he continues, "I've been worried sick about you all day. I'm so relieved to hear your voice. Other than thinking about you, I haven't accomplished a damn thing!"

Elin says straight out, "Oh, no? Doesn't this morning count for something? What the devil was that all about? And why were you at the Texaco petrol station?"

She draws a breath, realizing that she may be sounding a little harsh. Softening her tone, she says, "Just tell me that whatever was going on didn't involve me." Pausing a few seconds, she says, "I mean, it didn't . . . did it?"

Ramsay hesitates, searching for just the right words, "Look, Doll, let's leave it for later. Let me explain everything when I see you."

Only then does Ramsay realize that Elin has broken down and is weeping uncontrollably into the telephone. And, worst of all, except for words, he can't reach out over the phone to console her.

She's moaning, "First, my papa was murdered . . . and nobody will tell me why. Now, you're saying somebody is trying to kill me, too. Is that it? I mean, who knows what the hell to believe any more. It's a fucking web of insanity."

Alec Ramsay pauses, and then says, "Listen closely to me, Doll. Yes, those guys at the Texaco station intended you harm. Don't know who they were. And I don't know why they were there, except that they intended to kill you. At least one of them had a gun. And you had nothing, except your wits. Bottom line is this: They're both dead. And you're not!

"Maybe we'll never find out who they were, nor for whom they must have been working. But I'll bet you *The New York Times* will get it figured out before the Jersey police do."

"Look, Alec, I'll be okay," she says.

But Ramsay keeps on talking over her, "From what you've told me, this afternoon's deal at the clinic is just plain weird. I mean it's absolutely bizarre. Why on earth would a doctor hired to do a simple abortion want to kill you? It just doesn't compute."

"Makes no God-damned sense at all," he lies, remembering last night's phone call. "On the other hand, think about this. It's not every day that a man being primed to become the U.S. president has a child born out of wedlock."

"Oh, that's not fair," Elin tearfully interrupts, finally realizing that Ramsay now knows who Horatio really is. "Horatio is an upfront guy and he's my friend. He's not sinister. I know him too well. He just wouldn't do such an evil thing."

"I hear you, Doll. But people sometimes do strange and desperate things. You don't realize all the power that's at stake. Right now, you can't discount anything. Nor anybody."

Ramsay continues, "Can you picture a headline next November in *The Washington Post* or in the *Times* that reads, 'Humphrey elected U.S. President.' And then the next day there's a follow-up headline that says, 'Beautiful baby boy born to lovely Swedish girl knocked up by the newly elected president.'

"Hardly sounds like a textbook beginning to four great years as U.S. president. And then I can imagine a third headline: 'America's president resigns in disgrace and moves to Sweden.' Come to think of it, Doll, I can't think of a U.S. president who has ever had to resign in disgrace!"

Elin asks, "Alec, why did you say baby *boy* a moment ago?"

Ignoring her question, he says, "Now you stay put. I'm leaving for Washington right now . . . as soon as I shove my valise into the desk drawer."

Ramsay continues, "I'll fly the Eastern shuttle into National tonight, and then meet you at the ambassador's house. It's still on Nebraska, right?" Elin agrees.

"And, for Pete's sake, don't even think about going outside the house." Elin shudders when she hears the name "Pete." Not realizing that "Pete's sake" is an American colloquialism, she wonders how or what Alec Ramsay knows about Dr. Peter Moser. Does he know *everything*?

"Stay put, Elin. Stay warm. Be cool," says Ramsay in a deliberate cadence. "I'll get you out of Washington, and nobody will ever know you're gone. Nor will they know *where* you've gone. Dammit all, I don't know if we're on a secure line or not. Anyway, it's too late to worry about it. Let's stop jib-jawing, so I can get going to LaGuardia.

"Meanwhile, don't you worry about a thing, Doll. We'll get it all figured out . . . together."

Ramsay hangs up, and Elin can't believe she's lucky enough to have a friend like Alec. What's unresolved in her mind is whether he's lucky *good* or lucky *bad* for her.

◄ **C h a p t e r   3 0** ►

Treleavan Upbraids His Protégé in Ramsay's 14th Floor Office at JWT

Wednesday, May 15, 1968

Alec Ramsay's office, situated on the southwest corner of the 14th floor of the Graybar Building, is richly paneled in carved oak. The JWT archives do not record who first occupied this particular office, which includes a bathroom with huge white porcelain fixtures, but *he* must have been a powerhouse. And it must have been a man, Ramsay surmises, because in the early days there were precious few powerhouse females in Manhattan beyond writer-bon vivant Claire Boothe Luce and financial wizard Ruth Axe.

It's the same large office that Ramsay once shared with Gerry Broderick, the Pepsi Cola International account guy whose job responsibilities at JWT included having to gracefully handle occasional obscene phone calls and overt sexual propositions from Joan Crawford, the creepy sixty-something actress-wife of Pepsi-Cola's CEO. Evidently, Miss Crawford felt that Gerry, in his role as her husband's "agency guy," was an all-purpose tool.

Gerry never knew when Miss Crawford might call him, but his reaction was always the same, as he held his hand firmly over the receiver: "Oh shit, here we go. She's drunk again!"

More recently, Ramsay's officemate was Håkan Verner-Carlsson, who now heads up JWT's office in Stockholm. On Ramsay's credenza is an antique L.C. Smith typewriter that Verner-Carlsson always coveted, but he could never persuade

Alec to give him the vintage 1912 machine. Ramsay's consistent mantra was, "Sorry Håkan, old friend. Around here, one never knows when he may have to do his own typing. And so, my typewriter stays put!"

———

Ramsay's on the telephone when JWT's creative maven, Harry Treleavan, quietly slips into the office and inquires, "So, Alexander, what's up?" From past experience with Harry, Ramsay knows it's not a good conversation opener.

Ramsay, who has been "on hold" with Eastern Airlines, hangs up the receiver as Treleavan shuts the heavy oak door behind him. Ramsay starts a recitation of Elin's latest predicament.

"You know, Harry, I jumped into the sack with Elin a week before her dad died. So I figure her baby-in-waiting could just as easily be mine as the vice president's."

A light switches on in his brain, as Ramsay seemingly becomes enamored with this scenario. Ramsay looks closely at Treleavan's face for any telltale sign: Surprise, anger . . . for God's sake, any emotion at all!

Alec Ramsay senses Treleavan is on the verge of again losing his cool. And Old Harry doesn't disappoint, as he snaps: "It's high time that all of us on the team stop fucking around, both literally and figuratively. Goddamn it, Alec, we've got an election to win."

Ramsay shrivels up his forehead and nods, knowing that Treleavan is absolutely correct. But what can he say? Probably nothing! Yep, it's best not to say anything.

Treleavan raises his voice as he continues, "Each one of us needs to understand, once and for all, the enormity of the responsibility and opportunity that's been handed to us by Len Garment and Big John. We've all got to rededicate ourselves to getting Richard Nixon elected the 37th president of this republic.

"If . . . I mean *when* we pull it off, we'll all be in pig heaven for the rest of our days. None of us will ever have to do God-damned advertising again, unless it's on our own terms. We'll no longer be indentured to monosyllabic slave masters at Ford, Pan Am, RCA, Liggett & Myers, Kodak, Kellogg's, Pepsi or any of the rest. And, maybe best of all, we'll have that irrational, cigar-chewing, angry son-of-a-bitch, Lee Iacocca, out of our lives.

"Indeed," Treleavan continues, "when we reach Washington, the largest companies and organizations, JWT included, will become indentured to us. But this can happen only if we stay focused and single-minded, just like our client, Richard Nixon."

"We've got to get that fucking broad—damn, I can never remember her name—out of the country . . . and, thus, out of our collective hair. And I mean right now, not tomorrow, the next day or next week! She's become more than an irritant; she's a major distraction!

"For chrissakes," exclaims Treleavan, "maybe it would have been better all around if that doc in D.C. had finished her off. Then we would have had a doozie of a story that easily could be leaked to the press. Now, wouldn't *that* be ironic!"

Treleavan stands up and gazes out the window at the expanse of green oxidized copper roof that blankets Grand Central Station, far below Ramsay's office. He turns around and stares at Ramsay for a full four or five seconds, his face seeming to change expression several times before speaking again.

"Now you listen up carefully, Alec. Here's the deal, and it's the only deal on the table! I don't give a hoot whether you get on the phone and call some Republican mogul like Max Fisher in Detroit or a Democratic deep pocket like that Rädisson guy in

Minneapolis. Or even that Silverman fellow in Michigan . . . you know, the guy who all the New York papers are talking about because he's buying up all sorts of FLUXUS art crap here in New York and in Germany.

"The bottom line for you, my boy, is real simple. Make sure that Swedish heap of trouble is on a plane to a place far away . . . like by tomorrow night, latest! Give her some money; do whatever's necessary. Promise her anything. Tell her if she doesn't go, and go quietly—without a whimper—she's likely to wind up dead just like her old man. Alec, you gotta play hardball with that girl!

"And while we're having a friendly chat, young man, let me tell you something else. If she's not outta here, then you'd better be . . . 'cause your neck is on the line! I never want to hear what's-her-name's name ever mentioned again. End of chapter and book. Over and out! Do you get it? Now get out of here!"

Only then does Treleavan realize that it's he who is in Ramsay's office and, thus, is the one who must leave.

Without waiting for a response, Treleavan uses his fingers to pry open the ornate heavy oaken door, and slips out sideways.

Even before the door slowly swings shut, Ramsay picks up the telephone and redials Eastern Airlines. While waiting for somebody to answer, he reaches for his personal address book and flicks the pages open to "S," for Silverman.

◄ C h a p t e r   3 1 ►

Death and Trauma Stalk Government Leaders Worldwide

MAY 16 THROUGH JUNE 21, 1968

It hasn't been a good week anywhere around the globe. At least two-hundred thousand demonstrators have marched against the French government in Paris. Fighting has broken out against the government in South Yemen. The Viet Cong attack a U.S. Special Forces camp fifty-five miles from Saigon. And the AFL-CIO announced that it will suspend the UAW union unless it pays outstanding dues.

The International Red Cross appeals for emergency food relief for Biafra, and a Swedish count by the name of Carl Gustaf von Rosen starts a one-person crusade by using his small plane to fly food into Biafra.

Vice President Humphrey proclaims that "it's refreshing to see an individual take action when the United Nations and so many countries around the world seem anesthetized by inertia." American and Swedish citizens don't know about the merciful behind-the-scenes roles being enacted by the vice president and Sweden's prime minister.

In the Nebraska Republican presidential primary, former Vice President Richard Nixon wins 70 percent of the vote. On the Democratic side of the ledger, Senator Robert Kennedy defeats Senator Eugene McCarthy by 52–31 percent.

Soviet Premier Aleksei Kosygin arrives in Czechoslovakia on

May 17 for an official visit. Washington believes that Kosygin's visit is a precursor of an invasion.

On the same day, Israeli officials say that they insist upon the demilitarization of the Sinai Peninsula and the recognition of their country by the Arab states before they will return the captured territories. The United States conducts an underground nuclear test in the Nevada desert.

On May 18, Senator Robert Kennedy suggests that the South Vietnamese government begin negotiations with the National Liberation Front. President Johnson says that Kennedy must stop aiding the enemy.

The next day, May 19, an estimated ten thousand Czech students stage an anti-Soviet rally in Prague. And the Soviet Union agrees to help Pakistan build an electrical complex.

While U.S. troops battle North Vietnamese forces around Khe Sanh, the Americans for Democratic Action reaffirm their support of Senator Eugene McCarthy. In the midst of spreading strikes, French workers occupy the Paris Opera.

Reports from Bonn indicate that Hungarian CP First Secretary János Kádár has refused to participate in Warsaw Pact maneuvers near the Czechoslovak border.

And on May 20, most normal work activity in France grinds to a halt. Trains, planes and most public transportation no longer function. Shoppers feverishly stockpile provisions.

May 21 finds the United Nations Security Council adopting a resolution opposing Israel's administrative unification of the Jordanian and Israeli sector of Jerusalem. A landmine kills two Israeli farmers near the Gaza Strip. A Haitian Coast Guard vessel shells a small May 20 exile invasion force.

President Johnson asks Congress for a supplemental $3.9 billion for the Vietnam War.

Israeli Foreign Minister Abba Eban on May 22 says that Israel will ignore the May 21 United Nations resolution opposing the administrative unification of Jerusalem.

Civil disobedience continues in several countries. Five hundred student demonstrators occupy the Free University of Brussels. Violent street fighting between police and students erupts again in the Latin Quarter of Paris. An anti-Israeli demonstration takes place in the Gaza Strip. The small Haitian invasion force takes over a village near Cap-Haïtien.

Poor People's Campaign leader Jesse Jackson announces the evacuation of about two hundred inhabitants of the campaign's shanty-town, called Resurrection City, because of bad weather.

On May 25, Soviet Premier Aleksei Kosygin ends his consultations in Czechoslovakia amid reports that Warsaw Pact exercises will be held soon on Czech soil. The AP reports widespread civilian massacres in the Nigerian civil war.

Leaders of non-Negro groups in the Poor People's Campaign bitterly denounce the treatment they have received from Negro leaders. Senator Robert Kennedy proposes a $1 billion subsidized loan program to help businesses locate in rural and urban poverty areas.

A May 27 United Nations report says that the 1967 war, won by Israel, dealt a sharp setback to the economies of the Arab states. The same day, Israeli troops disperse demonstrating Arab high-school students in the Gaza Strip.

President Johnson orders U.S. Agriculture Secretary Orville Freeman to say that the May 21 CBS-TV documentary *Hunger in America* is a "one-sided and dishonest presentation."

Also on May 27, Morrow publishes Tom Wicker's *JFK and LBJ*.

On May 28, Israeli military authorities seal off the Gaza Strip to Arab traffic to counter anti-Israeli demonstrations. On the same day, Israel pays the United States more than $3 million in compensation for the sinking of the *U.S. Liberty* in the Mediterranean on June 8, 1967. This is a niggling amount compared to the many millions received annually from the U.S.

Senator Eugene McCarthy (45%) scores an upset victory over Senator Robert Kennedy (39%) in the Oregon Democratic presidential primary. And in Washington, D.C., police prevent one hundred and fifty demonstrators from the Poor People's Campaign from entering the U.S. Agriculture Department.

Cyrus Vance, U.S. peace negotiator at the Paris talks with North Vietnam, confers with President Johnson in the White House.

The AFL-CIO International Ladies' Garment Workers Union endorses Vice President Humphrey for president. To the candidate's chagrin, campaign workers at the Washington headquarters break out champagne.

On May 29, Israeli Foreign Minister Abba Eban says that Israel will only return the 1967 captured territories when the Arab states are ready to sign peace treaties with his country.

In a dramatic statement, Senator Robert Kennedy says that his candidacy will stand or fall on the results of the California primary. On the same day, lame-duck U.S. President Lyndon Johnson calls for the granting of the vote to eighteen-year-olds.

Before midnight on May 29, the *U.S. Scorpion* is reported missing. The American government refuses to release any details about the submarine.

May 30 news stories report that the United States has begun airlifting arms to Jordan. Israel's Washington lobby hollers foul, and initiates numerous one-on-one meetings with members of the U.S. Congress.

Increased fighting between South Vietnamese and Communist forces rages in the Cholon district of Saigon. Three to four hundred demonstrators from the Poor People's Campaign protest at the Supreme Court building on First Street in Washington, D.C.

The U.S. Supreme Court extends the right to trial by jury to criminal defendants in all but "petty" cases. The same day, May 30, former vice president Richard Nixon says that the U.S. Supreme Court has given a "green light to criminal elements" in the United States.

For the second time in two weeks, the U.S. Commander in South Vietnam, William Westmoreland, confers with President Johnson—this time at LBJ's ranch in Texas.

In Paris on May 31, North Vietnamese negotiators reject United States demands for military reciprocity in exchange for a halt to the bombing of North Vietnam.

Also on May 31, nearly five hundred demonstrators from the Poor People's Campaign take over an auditorium in the HEW Department and demand to meet with HEW Secretary Wilbur Cohen.

———

June 1968 starts with sad news from Westport, Connecticut: Deaf and blind writer Helen Keller dies at age eighty-seven.

On the same day, June 1, the Soviet Union launches Cosmos 223 . . . the USSR's twenty-second satellite launch in less than four months, when Cosmos 201 went skyward on February 6.

Police and students clash in Turin, Italy. Yugoslav students demonstrate in Belgrade for better living conditions.

South Vietnamese officials report that recent fighting in Saigon has resulted in 125,000 refugees.

And on June 3, the U.S. Supreme Court rules, 6–3, that jurors cannot be excluded from murder trial juries because of their objections to capital punishment. In another landmark decision the same day, the court rules that public school teachers cannot be dismissed for publicly criticizing school systems.

In the continuing saga of unprecedented civil disobedience in Washington, D.C., more than four hundred demonstrators from the Poor People's Campaign stage a seven-hour "camp-in" on the steps of the Justice Department. They demand to meet with U.S. Attorney General Ramsey Clark.

An actress shoots and critically wounds multi-millionaire Pop Art pioneer Andy Warhol in New York on June 3.

On June 4, Senator Robert Kennedy defeats Senator Eugene McCarthy in California's Democratic presidential primary. Earlier in the day, Attorney General Ramsey Clark meets with delegates from the Poor People's Campaign.

With encouragement from Vice President Humphrey, President Lyndon Johnson appeals to the Soviet Union to join the United States and other nations "in the spirit of Glassboro and Stockholm" to help achieve world peace. Meanwhile Israel and Jordan engage in a day-long clash near the Sea of Galilee, Viet Cong rockets strike Saigon and the surrounding area, and the Soviet Union launches Cosmos 224.

One day after winning the California Democratic presidential primary, New York's senator Robert Kennedy is seriously wounded in Los Angeles by a gunman. Senator Kennedy dies on June 6 of gunshot wounds inflicted by Sirhan Sirhan.

British journalist Randolph Churchill, the son of Sir Winston Churchill, dies in London at age fifty-seven.

On June 7, the body of Senator Robert Kennedy lies in state in St. Patrick's Cathedral in New York. In the afternoon, a Los Angeles grand jury hears testimony that an unidentified woman was seen talking to Robert Kennedy's assassin Sirhan

Sirhan seconds before the slaying took place.

The next day, June 8, Scotland Yard detectives arrest Martin Luther King Jr.'s alleged assassin, James Earl Ray, at Heathrow Airport in London.

During the June 8 Requiem Mass for the late Robert Kennedy, Senator Edward Kennedy delivers a eulogy in a strong but at times shaking voice in which he quotes his brother's favorite passage, "Some men see things as they are and say why. I dream of things that never were and say why not."

On the same day, June 8, Jordan reports that Saudi Arabia has pledged $36 million for arms purchases for the Jordanian army. Investigative reporters try to link this decision with RFK's assassin, Jordanian Sirhan Sirhan.

The same day, half the world away, the U.S. Commander in South Vietnam, General William Westmoreland, says that an allied military victory "in a classic sense" is impossible in Vietnam because of the self-imposed constraints limiting the U.S. war effort.

Acting in response to the murders of Martin Luther King, Jr. and Robert Kennedy, President Johnson's administration sends Congress its proposals to ban the mail-order sale of guns and ammunition. Also on June 10, the U.S. Supreme Court upholds the right of policemen to stop and frisk people for weapons.

On June 11, California Governor Ronald Reagan says that in most instances civil disorders have been encouraged by "demagogic" statements by prominent people. He refuses to cite specific examples.

Responding to a groundswell of support for an Edward Kennedy candidacy following his brother's murder in the ballroom of the Ambassador Hotel in downtown Los Angeles, close associates report on June 11 that he will neither run for the presidency nor accept a vice presidential nomination.

Vice President Humphrey isn't sure what to think when Senator Eugene McCarthy arrives at the White House on June 11 for a meeting with President Johnson. President Johnson also meets on the same day with the Shah of Iran.

On June 12, one day after meeting with President Johnson, Senator Eugene McCarthy announces the resumption of his presidential campaign. Also, Postmaster General Marvin Watson announces new postal requirements governing the mailing of firearms.

Reports leaking from the White House indicate that the United States has promised the Shah of Iran modern arms on easy credit terms.

While reports on June 13 indicate that South Vietnamese legislators are demanding the resumption of the bombing of North Vietnam, Senator Eugene McCarthy says that he thinks the U.S. public will accept a unilateral withdrawal of U.S. forces from Vietnam.

On June 15, the Kennedy family uses a brief television message to thank the American people for its expression of sympathy after the death of Robert Kennedy.

The New York Times on June 18 reports that the Israeli cabinet has agreed on a plan formulated by Labor Minister Yigal Allon calling for Israeli settlements in the West Bank along the Jordan River.

Senator Eugene McCarthy wins at least 52 of New York's 123 elected delegates in the state's Democratic primary. The Soviet Union launches Cosmos 227.

In London, Britain announces that it has withdrawn, for financial reasons, from a project for the construction of the world's largest atom smasher. Both Hubert Humphrey and Richard Nixon doubt the official reason provided by the British government, and issue separate press releases congratulating Britain on showing restraint in the proliferation of nuclear arms.

Following the lead of students at several U.S. colleges, Brazilian students seize a building on the University of Rio de Janeiro campus to protest poor education facilities and alleged United States interference in Brazilian education programs.

Under increasing pressure from *The New York Times* and *Washington Post*, the U.S. Defense Department reports that American combat deaths in Vietnam have risen above twenty-five thousand.

‹ Chapter 32 ›

Dr. Moser Gets a Dose of His Own Medicine

SATURDAY, JUNE 22, 1968

Saturday is the sunny second day of summer in suburban Arlington, Virginia. Flowers and tree leaves are popping after a cooler-than-usual spring. The lawns have greened up and already need regular cutting.

Citizens in Arlington couldn't care less that on this day Israeli Premier Levi Eshkol declares that the Jordan River must remain Israel's "security border" for all time, nor that Communist forces have mauled a South Vietnamese battalion outside of Saigon.

On this weekend, it wasn't unexpected news that Vice President Humphrey and Senator Eugene McCarthy were planning to appear separately before the Minnesota Democratic Party convention in St. Paul.

At 541 Arden Pond, the spacious red-brick colonial home with cream trim is getting burnished inside and out. Inside the house, Mrs. Peter Moser and her two daughters, ages thirteen and fifteen, have thrown open most windows and are methodically moving from room to room with a vacuum cleaner, a feather duster, dust rags and an assortment of furniture and glass polishes. Today the clean team is going all out at the Moser household!

On the side driveway, Dr. and Mrs. Moser's twelve-year-old son Tyson and three middle-school chums are shooting hoops against a white backboard mounted on a sturdy pole installed across the asphalt driveway from the cream-colored double garage door.

In the large front yard, Dr. Peter Moser has nearly finished his favorite Saturday morning chore, mowing and trimming the lawn. Most of the neighbors use the professional lawn care services which are so popular in suburban areas that surround D.C. Dr. Moser also engages a lawn service, but they work for him only on those weekends when he's out of town.

The good doctor claims that caring for his lawn and garden is a therapeutic and relaxing distraction from his hectic, although highly profitable, specialized medical practice in southwest Washington. Moreover, Dr. Moser knows he'll do a better job than anybody he can hire.

Except for an older-model gas-powered mower, he owns most of the same equipment used by the pros. Dr. Moser takes great pride in appearances and the quality of his work, whether he's at the clinic or at home.

It's almost lunchtime and Dr. Moser has been guiding his twenty-two-inch self-propelled mulching mower back and forth, back and forth for at least two hours. The cut pattern in the mowed grass resembles a miniature version of the outfield at Yankee Stadium, where young Peter Moser and a few buddies from the Bronx used to sneak into baseball games.

He's nearly finished mowing the front yard, with only the strip of grass left to do between the street and sidewalk.

———

Almost nobody in the neighborhood pays attention as a large green Ford pickup truck, fairly new and in good condition, cruises slowly down Dr. Moser's street for the second time in the last ten minutes. The driver seems to be searching for a particular address.

Indeed, he knows precisely what he's doing. It's Dr. Moser's house that's being surveilled!

At this same moment, behind the Safeway store two blocks away, two men have just about finished attaching a heavy device to the front of a large, dark blue, late-model Hertz rental sedan. The rig, bolted onto the bumper and frame, resembles the kind of device that police cars use to push disabled vehicles. Except that this one looks bigger and meaner.

Soon the green pickup truck doubles back to the Safeway and speeds across pavement on an angle toward two waiting men. The driver shouts to the men, who respond immediately by tossing their tools into the bed of the pickup. One guy then jumps into the car while the other one joins the driver in the pickup. Both vehicles retrace the route back to Arden Pond.

As the big, dark-colored sedan, a common sight on the streets of this quiet conservative neighborhood, slowly rounds the corner the driver spots his target. He pauses for a moment a few houses down the street until Dr. Moser makes his next turn around with the lawnmower and heads away from the waiting car.

Then, quickly accelerating to forty-five, and then to fifty-five miles per hour, the car begins its "run." With his back toward the oncoming car, the noise from the lawnmower's engine prevents Dr. Moser from hearing or sensing that a speeding vehicle is fast approaching. Moving very fast now, the driver runs his two right-hand wheels up over the neighbor's driveway slab, launching the car into the air at an awkward angle. The heavy car is airborne for just a split second.

When the car hits the ground, it smashes into Dr. Moser with enough force to send his body hurtling head-over-feet until it comes to rest limply on a lower limb of the giant 125-year-old spreading maple tree in the Moser front yard.

It's the same perfectly shaped tree—whose leaves each autumn almost magically turn into a wonderful festival of color—that first attracted Dr. and Mrs. Moser so many years before to their quiet, unassuming neighborhood. Another attractive feature about the neighborhood: there never was trouble of any kind.

With the driver struggling to regain control, the car careens down the street, fishtails around the corner and disappears. Ty Moser and his friends remain so engaged with their game of H-O-R-S-E that they fail to notice that Dr. Moser's badly damaged mowing machine, with its "drive" gear still engaged, has crossed the driveway and is cutting an erratic swath around the neighbor's front lawn.

Mrs. Moser chances to look out of an open window upstairs and sees deep tire tracks on her home's carefully manicured front lawn. Two shoes are lying under the old maple tree.

She screams, and then yells in her unique, unusually high-pitched voice, "Girls, come quickly. Your father's had an accident."

The widow Moser doesn't yet know the half of it!

◄ Chapter 33 ►

Democratic and Republican Presidential Candidates
Parry for Political Advantage

JUNE 23 THROUGH NOVEMBER 1, 1968

Nothing has been "business as usual" in 1968, except for growing levels of rancor and nastiness displayed in the political campaigns of the men [indeed, where are the women in this scenario?] seeking to represent their parties in the U.S. presidential election on Tuesday, November 5. The only sure bet seems to be that Richard Nixon will be the Republican candidate.

On the Democratic side, McCarthy and Humphrey are fighting tooth and nail for convention delegate votes. Probably the better of the candidates, Hubert Humphrey is handicapped by his service and apparent loyalty to President Lyndon Baines Johnson.

Both inside and out of the United States, foment continues in every direction . . . fed by the unpopular war in Vietnam. There are no easy answers, and most certainly none of the potential four candidates are offering any!

Hoping to attract young people to vote the Democratic ticket, President Johnson asks Congress to approve a constitutional amendment to lower the voting age to eighteen.

In a front-page story on June 30, Democratic Senator McCarthy says that it's conceivable that he could back New York Republican Governor Nelson Rockefeller for the U.S. presidency over Vice President Humphrey. People are saying that not only is McCarthy a "crybaby," he's also remarkably disloyal to the political party that's brought him considerable national fame and personal fortune.

On July 3, President Johnson, citing a sniper slaying in New York's Central Park earlier in the day, calls for gun-control legislation. Although he doesn't say so, Johnson knows he wouldn't be the U.S. president if it wasn't for an illegal rifle in the hands of an assassin. A key congressional leader, Representative Carl Albert (D-Okla), states his opposition to all major gun control bills.

At a July Fourth celebration, California Governor Ronald Reagan says that many U.S. citizens carry guns "because they have lost faith in the American government's ability to protect them." On the same day, Vice President Humphrey is heckled by anti-war demonstrators during a speech in Philadelphia.

Richard Nixon privately tells key staffers that he thinks that the unbalanced United States support of Israeli interests over those of the Palestinians will one day come back to haunt America in ways that cannot even be imagined.

President Lyndon Johnson is distressed to learn that Atheneum has published Hugh Sidey's *A Very Personal Presidency*. Also of concern to the Johnson administration, for unspecified reasons, is the fact that a U.S.-owned newspaper, the *International Herald Tribune*, goes on sale in Moscow for the first time in forty years.

Controversial South Vietnamese President Nguyen Van Thieu says on July 10 that he may authorize the U.S. to begin withdrawal of soldiers in 1969. Both Vice President Humphrey and former Vice President Nixon ask the question: "Wait a minute, who's running this show . . . Vietnam or the United States?"

In a seemingly direct challenge to U.S. President Lyndon Johnson, Vice President Hubert Humphrey, former Vice President Nixon and New York's Republican Governor Nelson Rockefeller propose on July 13 a Vietnam peace plan. The U.S. State Department immediately accuses Rockefeller of "meddling."

On July 18, former U.S. President Dwight Eisenhower endorses Richard Nixon for the Republican presidential nomination. Potential candidate Nelson Rockefeller fails to heed advice by his advisors to pull out of the race and throw his support behind Nixon.

Saddam Hussein's puppet Foreign Minister Nasir el-Hani says that Iraq will not resume relations with the United States. Late in the afternoon of July 21, Hubert Humphrey is said to have been heard muttering "Oh, oh!"

At the Governors' Conference in Cincinnati, President Johnson tries to defend his Vietnam policy. At the same moment, Senator Eugene McCarthy is telling a press conference that President Johnson is "inflexible" on Vietnam. Hubert Humphrey's strategy is to lie low while other potential candidates absorb the *flak*! So far, his plan has worked pretty well.

New York Governor Nelson Rockefeller says that the long-term foreign policy goal of the United States should be to shift "from a relationship of conflict to one of cooperation with the Soviet Union." Some are touting Rockefeller for the Nobel Peace Prize just for daring to make the suggestion!

Democratic U.S. Senator Edward Kennedy announces on July 26 that he will not accept the Democratic vice presidential nomination. It's unclear as to whether Vice President Hubert Humphrey made an offer to Kennedy, but what seems clear to Harry Treleavan, Alec Ramsay and others on Nixon's team is that without Kennedy, Humphrey cannot win the presidency in 1968!

Republicans rejoice upon hearing that a Gallup Poll shows Richard Nixon ahead of major Democratic candidates. Within hours, Democrats rejoice when told that a Harris Poll shows Nixon *trailing* major Democrat candidates!

The Republican National Convention opens in Miami, Florida. Former Vice President Nixon, John Mitchell and campaign team members from J. Walter Thompson hold last-minute strategy meetings in a large hotel room.

At the convention, the 1968 Republican platform stresses the need for an honorable negotiated peace in Vietnam. In an attempt to unsettle the convention, looting breaks out in Miami's Negro areas, and police arrest fifty-two persons.

But the big news on this day, August 8, is that **Richard Nixon wins the Republican Party's nomination for U.S. president and Maryland Governor Spiro Agnew is selected to be his running mate**. Within the Nixon camp, there is a general view that Agnew will not be a high-quality candidate; but that—although now stuck with Agnew—Nixon will be a strong enough candidate to win on his own merits.

U.S. Senator George McGovern (D-S.D.) announces that he is an active candidate for the Democratic presidential nomination. McGovern confides to close associates that he thinks Humphrey will win the nomination at the Chicago convention, but that Nixon is a shoo-in to beat Humphrey. In McGovern's mind, this means that he (McGovern) is almost assured of being the Democrats' choice to run in 1972.

Lame-duck U.S. President Lyndon Johnson is unwilling to support McGovern, Humphrey or any other Democrat who may be nominated. Curiously, Johnson decides to give a detailed briefing on world affairs to Republican nominees Nixon and Agnew.

On August 19, U.S. President Johnson says that the United States will make no further moves to de-escalate the Vietnam War until North Vietnam makes a serious move toward peace. Immediately following Johnson's statement, Senator George McGovern says that there must be a massive de-escalation of the Vietnam War!

Vice President Hubert Humphrey calls off his scheduled

debate with Senator Eugene McCarthy. Speculation suggests that Humphrey doesn't wish to get "sideways" with President Johnson just prior to the Democratic National Convention in Chicago.

Finally, the convention opens in a tense atmosphere. Chicago police use tear gas to disperse three thousand anti-war demonstrators and make 140 arrests.

On August 28, the Democratic National Convention nominates U.S. Vice President Hubert Humphrey as its 1968 presidential candidate as violent street battles between police and students rage in Chicago.

The next day, August 29, the Democratic National Convention nominates Senator Edmund Muskie of Maine as its vice presidential candidate. Pundits warn that things do not look rosy for the Democratic ticket in 1968. One reason: U.S. senators most often are considered unelectable because they lack executive experience. A notable exception was JFK's narrow victory in 1960 over former U.S. Vice President Richard Nixon, an election that many still claim was bought and paid for by Kennedy's father.

On September 4, Republican presidential candidate Richard Nixon draws an enthusiastic and orderly crowd in Chicago. It's almost the antithesis of crowd behavior just a week earlier during the Democratic convention, when mobs were rioting on the streets of Democratic Mayor Richard Daley's Chicago!

On September 8, U.S. Vice President Hubert Humphrey resorts to borderline name-calling when he describes former U.S. Vice President Richard Nixon as "sort of a Cold War warrior."

Highlighting his ongoing disagreements with Richard Nixon and Lyndon Johnson regarding the Vietnam "conflict," Vice President Humphrey says that the United States can start to remove troops from South Vietnam in late 1968 or early 1969. The Democratic presidential candidate's suggestion is received by

Congress and others with deafening "silence!"

A Gallup Poll released on September 10 reports that 50 percent of the union members interviewed in the South favor George Wallace over Humphrey (29%) or Nixon (16%). A majority of Nixon's labor support appears to be Teamsters-related, inasmuch as union boss James R. Hoffa has already signaled that he favors the Republican former vice president!

Republican presidential nominee Richard Nixon calls for the suspension of aid and credits to all countries dealing with North Vietnam.

Richard Nixon's inability to select competent people is again highlighted when his hand-picked Republican vice presidential candidate, Spiro Agnew, uses the word "Polack" in referring to Americans of Polish ancestry. Hubert Humphrey's election team gets busy trying to figure out how to take advantage of Agnew's predilection to "shoot off his mouth!"

Reports on September 14 indicate that U.S. President Johnson has decided against selling Israel fifty F-4 Phantom jet fighters for the time being.

On September 15, directly countering his boss's position, U.S. Vice President Hubert Humphrey says that the U.S. should immediately sell F-4 military jets to Israel. When asked "why?" by a stringer for *Time* magazine, Humphrey turns around and briskly walks away! Evidently the vice president chooses to answer only those questions that come with easy answers!

U.S. Vice President Hubert Humphrey on September 18 urges immediate Senate ratification of the nuclear nonproliferation treaty.

And here are two more *flashes* from outer space: The Soviet Union lunar probe flies around the moon, while the United States fails to place its latest communications satellite into synchronous orbit.

On September 19, Vice President Hubert Humphrey says that he will make peace in Vietnam his chief goal *if* [not *when*] he is elected president. Meanwhile, over in the White House, President Johnson again calls for a "sustained effort in Vietnam." Clearly, President Johnson's statements are not helping Humphrey's campaign. It almost seems as if the president wishes for the Republican candidate to defeat Humphrey!

On September 20, Republican presidential nominee Richard Nixon draws an impressive crowd in downtown Philadelphia, while an elated John Mitchell congratulates both himself and J. Walter Thompson's campaign-team members.

The next day, September 21, Big John is singing a different tune after Republican vice presidential candidate Spiro Agnew uses the term "fat Jap" while referring to a reporter of Japanese ancestry. First, it's Agnew's September 13 "Polack" reference to people of Polish ancestry, and now this crude remark. The Nixon people are desperate to find a way to muzzle Agnew, who repeatedly has demonstrated his lack of sound judgment in making public pronouncements!

Also on September 21, anti-war hecklers disrupt Vice President Humphrey's speech in Cleveland. He reminds them that he's been "*against* the war," but they persist because Humphrey's boss continues to be "*for* the war!" Later, the vice president confides to his aide-de-camp, Lawrence Gartner, that he's "totally frustrated, and sorry I got into this messy presidential sweepstakes!"

Republican vice presidential candidate Spiro Agnew apologizes for his use of the terms "Polack" and "fat Jap." A new Harris Poll says that, despite Agnew, Nixon is leading Humphrey by 39–31 percent.

Vice President Humphrey promises to "reassess the entire situation in Vietnam, if elected." Once again, Humphrey seems tentative in his statements regarding Vietnam and his odds for victory.

In a carefully calculated political move, Republican presidential candidate Richard Nixon says on September 24 that he opposes reducing the number of U.S. troops in Vietnam. The Republican presidential nominee repeats his charge that Vice President Humphrey's talk of an early return of some U.S. troops from Vietnam might undermine the U.S. negotiation position in the Paris peace talks.

Democratic vice presidential candidate Edmund Muskie invites an anti-war heckler to share the podium at Washington & Jefferson College.

U.S. Ambassador to the United Nations George Ball on September 26 resigns to join the Humphrey presidential campaign.

On September 27, about one hundred and fifty anti-war demonstrators disrupt a Humphrey rally in Seattle, Washington. Humphrey pouts to Gartner, "Why don't they ever give Nixon trouble? After all, he's the hawk in their henhouse!"

On September 30, Vice President Humphrey says that—if elected president—he will stop the bombing of North Vietnam if it agrees to restore the demilitarized zone. The Nixon people smile because they know Humphrey's messages are not getting the media coverage needed to register a bump in the polls.

On October 3, presidential candidates Nixon and Humphrey reject the use of nuclear weapons in Vietnam. In a supplementary statement, Republican candidate Nixon says that George Wallace "isn't fit to be president" because of some of his extreme positions. For example, opines Nixon, "Mr. Wallace is said to prefer *doggie style* to the *missionary position.*"

U.S. officials publicly quote Cambodian leaders admitting for the first time that Communist forces are using Cambodian territory for attacks on South Vietnam. The Democratic presidential nominee, Hubert Humphrey, is overheard telling Larry Gartner, "See, I told you those doggone Communists aren't fighting fair!"

On October 4, the liberal activist group Americans for Democratic Action endorses the Humphrey-Muskie ticket for 1968.

And on October 6, *The New York Times* endorses Vice President Humphrey's candidacy for U.S. president in 1968. This is not a surprise! [Dwight Chapin, Ron Ziegler and Alec Ramsay know that various *Times* reporters have been shadowing Richard Nixon's every move since early February 1968. In fact, it was Dwight Chapin who invited *Times* political writer Tom Wicker to speak in early 1967 to a group of executives at a management luncheon in J. Walter Thompson's tenth-floor dining room. During the post-luncheon Q&A session, Nixon team members—including Chapin, Ramsay and Harry Treleavan—were able to ask questions that drew out Wicker's feelings about Nixon and other possible presidential candidates. Wicker never conveyed a realization, then or later, that he had been set-up.]

———

On October 7, Democratic vice presidential candidate Edmund Muskie's criticism of independent presidential candidate George Wallace is greeted by stone silence at the International Association of Iron Workers' convention.

Also on October 7, a *New York Times* survey published less than one month ahead of the 1968 election indicates that the Democrats will maintain control of the Congress despite Republican gains.

Senator Eugene McCarthy says on October 8 he will support Vice President Humphrey for president *only* if he accepts a new government in South Vietnam and new reforms for the Democratic Party.

On October 9, mounted policemen in Washington, D.C., break up a group of about four hundred anti-war demonstrators awaiting the arrival of Vice President Humphrey, who has just rejected Senator Eugene McCarthy's conditions for his support.

An Australian court rules that an accused murderer is insane because he has an extra Y chromosome. Vice President Humphrey laughingly suggests to his chief-of-staff, Larry Gartner, that perhaps George Wallace also has a chromosomal abnormality.

Republican presidential nominee Richard Nixon says that western European countries should carry more of their own defense burden.

In mid-October, Republican presidential candidate Richard Nixon says that the United States should begin moving toward *volunteer* armed forces. Noting the large number of eligible—and presumably intelligent—men who have fled to Canada and elsewhere to escape Vietnam military service, some pundits claim that Nixon's idea of an all-volunteer army will ensure that the United States has a "dumbed-down" army. They believe, "only under-educated, incompetent and otherwise unemployable persons will opt to join the military."

Republican vice presidential candidate Spiro Agnew continues his verbal assault on American sensibilities by saying, "To some extent, if you've seen one city slum you've seen them all." Clearly, the Nixon team hasn't been able to muffle Agnew's simplistic—and often ignorant—public declarations!

On October 19, Republican presidential candidate Richard Nixon repeats that the United States should encourage the formation of regional defense associations in order to lessen the need of direct United States intervention. The Democratic presidential nominee continues to be uncommonly quiet regarding a variety of issues. Some in the press are starting to suggest that Hubert Humphrey has "lost focus." Indeed, it's past mid-October and the Humphrey-Muskie team is running out of time!

Democratic presidential nominee Hubert Humphrey's campaign office issues a statement supporting birth control. By again delaying for too long an important position statement, Humphrey strikes many Democratic and independent voters as being more of a *follower* than a *leader*.

An October 21 Gallup Poll shows Richard Nixon leading Hubert Humphrey by 43–31 percent. This seems like an astounding margin only two weeks before the November 5 presidential election.

On October 24, Republican presidential candidate Richard Nixon rejects the notion of "parity," or equality, of nuclear forces between the Soviet Union and the United States.

President Johnson signs a bill increasing penalties for possession of illegal drugs.

President Johnson says that the United States is still waiting for a reply from North Vietnam promising a de-escalation of the war in return for a complete halt of the United States bombing.

Showing how fast a "quickie" book can be written and published, World Publishing releases Norman Mailer's *Miami and the Siege of Chicago*, which covers the 1968 Republican and Democratic conventions.

On October 26, President Johnson attacks the Republicans as "wooden soldiers of the status quo." Democratic Party big-wigs, including Andrew Gallagher Ryan, scratch their heads wondering what Johnson is really trying to say. Some think that their president must be looking in his mirror!

Republican U.S. presidential candidate Richard Nixon says that he is against imposing a coalition government in South Vietnam. Editorial writers are saying that whether you agree or not with Nixon isn't the point; what's important is his attempt to communicate ideas to voters. A backlash is setting in against Humphrey, who invariably seems overly concerned that he may offend someone. Meanwhile, Humphrey's key advisors repeatedly say it's impossible for him to be "all things to all people!"

Civil-rights leader Dr. Ralph Abernathy on October 28 endorses Vice President Humphrey for U.S. president. The question is being asked, "Who else would Abernathy support, and why has he waited until the last week of the campaign to speak out in favor of Humphrey?"

President Johnson confers in Washington with General Creighton Abrams, new supreme commander of U.S. forces in South Vietnam. Like wartime military leaders tend to do, Abrams tells his president that things are going well. But Johnson knows intuitively that Abrams is wrong!

On October 29, Senator Eugene McCarthy finally endorses Vice President Humphrey for U.S. president. For Humphrey, it's probably too little, and quite likely too late!

President Johnson announces that he is suspending the bombing of North Vietnam as of November 1. To some observers, it seems like a last-minute attempt to curry favor with voters on behalf of Democratic presidential nominee Hubert Humphrey.

On the heels of President Johnson's announcement, candidates Nixon, Humphrey and Wallace support the President's decision to stop the bombing of North Vietnam.

◄ Chapter 34 ►

At the Final Pre-Election Pow-Wow at Nixon's Campaign Headquarters, John Mitchell Sets-the-Stage for a Future Republican Political Disaster

SATURDAY, NOVEMBER 2, 1968

Sunny, blue-skied Saturday afternoons in November are special to lovers in Manhattan—both heterosexual and otherwise—who stroll hand-in-hand along Park Avenue.

But not everyone can be outside taking the air on November 2, this last Saturday afternoon before the 1968 U.S. presidential election.

Indeed, Big John Mitchell has gathered a handful of his players around the large table in the main conference room of the Nixon campaign headquarters. Why? So Mitchell can convey last-minute polling results while also double-checking media communications planning for Sunday, Monday and Election Day on Tuesday, November 5. Also on the agenda are two or three last-minute changes in Mr. Nixon's pre-election schedule, plus some related staffing assignments.

Mitchell also intends to cover an *off-agenda* item that has just come to his attention via a handwritten note from campaign gate-keeper Dick Garbutt. Garbutt's message conveys information and some apparent substantiating evidence regarding an allegation about a shocking and alleged adulterous indiscretion by Nixon's opponent, Democratic presidential nominee Hubert Humphrey. Garbutt says that the info was given to him late Saturday morning by a stranger who had called his office and asked if he could stop by with something important.

Harry Treleavan and Alec Ramsay are in the campaign war room with Mitchell, Frank Shakespeare, Dick Garbutt, Len Garment, Dwight Chapin, Ruth Jones, Al Scott and a couple of other worthies. Trolling in the hallway outside the closed door is Theodore White, who claims he is close to wrapping up the manuscript for his newest book, to be entitled *The Making of the President—1968*.

After dealing with the latest overnight polling data and a few housekeeping matters, Big John segues into the off-agenda topic.

Mitchell quietly and matter-of-factly comments that only recently he has received privileged information about a young Swedish woman named Elin Lindström, a twenty-something female acquaintance of Nixon's opponent. Recently she has been spotted walking on Marstrand Island, along Sweden's West Coast.

Shakespeare murmurs, "Yeah, so what's new, John? Jack Kennedy's old girlfriends can be spotted almost every day on the streets of Boston, Washington and Las Vegas."

"I'll tell you '*what's new*,' Frank!" With his voice growing more strident, Big John speaks with emphasis: "This honey's heavy with child! And we think she's probably ready to *drop* it any day now."

Ramsay and Treleavan are expressionless as they furtively glance sideways until their knowing eyes connect.

Mitchell continues, "And furthermore, I have it on good authority that this woman is carrying the vice president's baby. And we think the kid was conceived in Stockholm back in early February, just after Al-Wahid's kid screwed things up by mistakenly killing this woman's father instead of Humphrey!"

The instant these last words had left his brain and passed his lips, Mitchell realizes he has made an egregious error. But it's too late to take back his words!

Paying no attention to the collective gasp around the table, an even more agitated Mitchell now snaps, "Look, none of you heard that, understand? I mean, forget it! Everyone! It simply didn't happen!"

And then, contrary to his usually measured counsel, Mitchell continues to grow more irate and irrational. His demeanor is highly animated and his voice grows louder.

He finally bellows, "Humphrey's baby! How's it possible nobody here knew about this before now? Are we all so cloistered that we don't hear anything from the outside world? You know, like from the real world? Or are we all just too dumbed-down to recognize the obvious?"

Big John turns on Alec Ramsay. "Ramsay, Garbutt here says you know this dame we're talking about." Dick Garbutt looks straight ahead, avoiding Ramsay's direct stare. "Certainly *you* must have known she's been fucking Humphrey. He's vice president of the United States, for God's sake!"

Mitchell pauses for an instant to catch his breath. "Holy Christ and four-hands-around, even I know the babe got screwed by Kennedy seven years ago in the utility room next to the White House pool."

Ramsay's face drains. Growing wiser with each moment, he chooses to remain silent. Anyway, there's nothing Ramsay can say now that will mollify Mitchell's by now towering, red-faced rage.

"Scumpy shit," Big John continues. "It all adds up. But obviously none of you geniuses ever passed basic arithmetic! Chrissakes, whose side are you guys on, anyway?" he asks accusatorily while scanning the eyes of everyone in the room.

Mitchell knows full well that his captive audience is flummoxed and is fast growing tired of his act. But he's determined to press onward, despite all the work that needs to done between now and Tuesday morning when the polls open across America and then west across the Pacific to Hawaii and Guam.

"This election race is so unbelievably tight. Just look for yourself. The numbers on that chart tell the story. And here we are, sitting atop a news story that has the power to obliterate our opponent. It's a story with power to metaphorically assassinate old Hubert . . . to do, in a completely oblique manner, what those assholes failed to do in Stockholm."

Big John hesitates momentarily to again survey the faces around the table. "But now, it's simply too late to use our information! Why? Because, dammit, it's the last weekend before the election . . . that's why! No news editor will go with a story this big when there's no time to check it out!

"We know Humphrey is speaking in Texas tomorrow, and then in Los Angeles on Monday. He's got the big-time press on his side, and it's simply too late to do a number on the guy . . . whether or not this baby thing is really true.

"Frankly, now I don't care one way or the other. It's just too damn late," Big John shouts with a tinge of hopelessness and desperation.

"We've simply run out of time and there's nothing we can do. Anything we might try now will just get us lynched by Tom Wicker and his fellow travelers.

"They'll simply be dismissive of any charge that's made. They'll call it a last-minute desperation pass by Nixon. It won't hurt Humphrey one whit, but the TV and newspaper people will pull out the stops to do a last-minute crucifixion of the Old Man. Any credibility we've built up for him will evaporate in one eye blink."

Mitchell continues to repeat himself. "No time left for the knuckle-dragging newsies to check out the story. Even if we give them everything we have, they just won't use it. Maybe later they would, but not in time to help us win on Tuesday."

Ruth Jones starts to pipe up, but she's steam rollered by Mitchell, who continues, "And, anyway, the Old Man himself wouldn't let us go with this story now. He'll think it's a bad joke . . . a terrible idea that will give dirty tricks a bad name.

Although a few folks around the table think Mitchell is cooling off a bit, they're wrong! Boy, are they wrong. No question that his anger is restoking toward another crescendo!

And Big John's repeating himself. He rails on about the close-ness of the race and about how this campaign needs more than a little advantage, legitimate or not. Everything is crucial to helping assure Nixon's victory.

"Ultimately," he claims, "We're in a business where fractions and missed opportunities count for everything. And we've just missed-out on one huge opportunity!"

Mitchell swivels back toward Ruth Jones, and asks what's on her mind. She shakes her head sideways, deciding that right now there's greater merit in being seen instead of heard.

Big John continues, unabated, "We've screwed up, we're really fucked." He screams, "This royal opportunity to screw Humphrey is wasted! Failure of this magnitude is unacceptable and, I guarantee you, will never happen again!"

Complete silence prevails, except for the din of traffic horns on the streets far below.

Another thought strikes Big John. "You can bet the farm that those Democrats have plenty of secrets locked up in their heads and file drawers. I don't know yet how we get to them, but we need to get it figured out. How do we get their G2 early, and turn it to our advantage?

"Maybe we need to start taking hostages, and torture them. No, that's what Democrats do! Republicans typically want to avoid unnecessary confrontation. So maybe the answer lies some-where in between: Simply break into their offices, and take the files we want!

"*If*—and all of you should be praying this happens—rather I should say *when* the Old Man beats Humphrey three days from now, all of us will be in the driver's seat for at least four years. And chances are good it'll be eight!"

Big John looks in Treleavan's direction. "And I can promise you that Harry, here, will start next Wednesday morning thinking about what needs to be done to set-the-duck for Nixon's 1972 re-election campaign and victory.

"When re-election time rolls around in '72, we will not—repeat *not*—have left anything to chance. Nothing! Do you hear me?" he yells. "Just do it," he screams, looking at nobody in particular, but meaning *everyone* in particular!

Mitchell's now cracking up. He's completely out of control, maybe even berserk. All eyes follow as he walks over to the side of the room and reaches for a Wilson softball bat, one of several that the Nixon campaign team has used sporadically for pick-up games with press people in Central Park.

Without warning, Big John Mitchell swings the bat with all his strength . . . knocking over the pile of metal folding chairs stacked neatly against the wall. One chair flips end-over-end and shatters a window, sending shards of glass streaking onto the Park Avenue sidewalk below.

The room falls totally silent . . . again. Ramsay, who is surprised as much by Big John's upper-body strength as by his irrational action, ponders for only a split second the possible consequences of what he's about to do.

Deciding to go for it, Alec Ramsay cups both hands around his mouth and proclaims in his best Ernie Harwell baseball announcer's voice, "Fans, it seems improbable, but it's true. The *son-of-a-Mitch* has cleared the window and hit it clear outta the park.

I mean, clear *onto* Park. Park Avenue, that is!"

No one smiles.

Except Big John Mitchell, who can't restrain himself from laughing out loud!

With that, Big John abruptly turns toward the door and calmly proclaims, "Okay, now let's all clear out of here and get back to work. We're gonna win this thing Tuesday!"

◄ **C h a p t e r   3 5** ►

Contentious Events Threaten to Upstage the November 5th U.S. Presidential Election

Nᴏᴠᴇᴍʙᴇʀ 2 ᴛʜʀᴏᴜɢʜ Nᴏᴠᴇᴍʙᴇʀ 5, 1968

On November 2, Egyptian President Gamal Nasser announces the formation of a civil guard to defend against Israeli commando attacks west of the Suez Canal.

Israeli authorities impose a curfew in Bethlehem for the first time since the city's capture during the June 1967 war.

The New York Times reports that two thousand Jews have emigrated from Poland since March 1968. But no one seems able to report where they've gone!

A consensus is growing that Vice President Humphrey is rapidly narrowing the gap between himself and Richard Nixon. This belief seems to be confirmed by reports that Nixon's campaign chief "nearly went berserk" in a November 2nd morning closed-door meeting at campaign headquarters on Park Avenue in Manhattan. Big John Mitchell tells his wife, Martha, that he's determined to find the "sneaky leaker."

The Dutch Roman Catholic episcopate upholds the Dutch bishops' decision leaving use of artificial contraceptives up to the individual. The Vatican quickly expresses its "abject disgust."

South Vietnamese President Nguyen Van Thieu announces that his government will not attend the Paris peace talks if the National Liberation Front is represented by a separate delegation.

———

Smelling the possibility of victory for the first time, Democratic presidential nominee Hubert Humphrey goes to Texas on November 3 for an unscheduled speech. An enthusiastic crowd of fifty-eight thousand hears Humphrey and heartily applauds his message. The candidate tells Gartner that he is "thrilled" with his reception in Lyndon Johnson's Texas.

Jordanian soldiers and Palestinian commandos clash near Amman. King Hussein is highly upset upon learning that Arabs are fighting Arabs!

Fifty thousand Greeks defy martial law and demonstrate in central Athens against the government.

A U.S. plane in Vietnam accidentally bombs a Marine Corps unit, killing six Marines.

On Monday, November 4, Hubert Humphrey goes to Los Angeles for another unscheduled event. Almost magically, one-hundred thousand enthusiastic people show up to hear Humphrey's speech. His advisors select Los Angeles because of the three-hour time difference provided by Pacific Standard Time, plus the fact that Los Angeles is a prime media center which can provide major headlines back East bright and early on Election Day morning, November 5.

Jordanian security forces suppress an anti-government demonstration of ten thousand.

Peruvian newspapers stage a twenty-four-hour general strike to protest against recent press restrictions.

Left-wing students occupy administration buildings at San Fernando Valley State College in Greater Los Angeles.

———

On November 5, Richard Milhous Nixon is narrowly elected 37th President of the United States. It may be the closest margin of victory ever in a U.S. presidential election!

Student disturbances take place at George Washington University, Washington, D.C.

Israeli Prime Minister Levi Eshkol declares that Israel considers the Jordan River as its security frontier in any peace agreement it might negotiate with Jordan.

◄ Chapter 36 ►

*The News Anchor at Sweden's Government-Controlled
TV Studio in Stockholm Headlines the Fates of
Richard Nixon, Tariq Al-Wahid, and Elin Lindström*

WEDNESDAY, NOVEMBER 6, 1968

On Stockholm's east side, multiple television monitors line a
studio wall in the main news facility at the Swedish Broadcasting
Company.

One screen shows the day and date: "*Onsdag, 6 November 1968.*"
Another screen shows Richard Nixon with both arms thrust into
the air, with the index and middle fingers on both hands forming
his trademark "V for Victory." The words "Washington, D.C."
are superimposed on the lower part of the screen. The camera
zooms in on the Nixon scene. The announcer's Swedish audio is
enhanced by English subtitles.

Images on two other monitor screens are less well defined.

Swedish Broadcasting's news anchor, Bengt Goransson, edito-
rializes in his perfectly modulated anchorman's baritone, "Ah, it
seems that the new American president believes that if the 'V'
sign was good enough for British statesman Winston Churchill,
then it's good enough for Richard Nixon. And two 'Vs' are even
better! One can only hope that Mr. Nixon knows which way his
palms should face! It does make a big difference, you know!"

The Swedish broadcaster continues, "In yesterday's national
election in the United States, Republican Richard Milhous Nixon
became America's 37th president. He beat the Democrat, Hubert
Horatio Humphrey, by the narrowest of voting margins. It was

almost a mirror image of the 1960 election in which America's beloved John F. Kennedy defeated Mr. Nixon by only a few thousand votes, many of them allegedly cast by dead people resurrected for the occasion by Chicago's legendary Democratic Mayor Richard Daley."

Goransson drones on, spouting more of his country's liberal dogma. "All Sweden is saddened today by the election loss of its favorite American friend and political soulmate of Sweden's Premier Tage Erlander and his anointed successor, Olof Palme.

"Swedes were hoping for a Humphrey victory yesterday because, as ex-officio president of the free world, it was anticipated that Humphrey would draw Sweden and America closer together than ever before. Unlike President Johnson before him, Hubert Humphrey could be depended upon to shut down the horrible Vietnam War that continues to ravage American interests at home and abroad."

The screen dissolves to a scene showing a body bag being loaded onto a khaki-colored Russian-built military utility vehicle parked outside of a mud and stone building. *"Near Damascus, Syria"* is superimposed over the scene.

The announcer intones, "This morning a Syrian military team, reportedly acting on information supplied to U.S. authorities by Robert Kennedy's alleged assassin, Sirhan Sirhan, found a nearly mummified male corpse chained to a bed in a mud building southeast of Khirbet An-Nbash and Damascus. Circumstances surrounding discovery of the body are being withheld, although the body is thought to have lain undiscovered for several months.

"Authorities are said to be investigating a weird mystery within a mystery. They are puzzled as to why the dead man's penis has been tied off with a tightly knotted bright red ribbon."

The screen dissolves to the scene being displayed on a third screen in the studio . . . showing a young woman holding a newborn infant. She looks haggard and drained. And with an unflattering do-it-yourself haircut framing sad eyes and a red nose, she is not particularly attractive. The lady obviously has been through a rough patch, and seems in need of rest and perhaps even medical or psychological attention.

"Uddevalla Hospital" is superimposed over the scene. The hospital is located in a medium-sized industrial seacoast town an hour north of Göteborg.

"Moving to our next story," says Goransson, "In the West Coast city of Uddevalla, Miss Elin Lindström is shown leaving the hospital's west wing birthing center with her newborn son, Erik. Miss Lindström is unmarried and is the only daughter of the late, popular Swedish journalist Lars Lindström. You may remember that Lindström was mysteriously murdered last February outside the Grand Hotel by a still unidentified gunman, who was later found dead in the Stockholm suburb of Näcka."

The television monitor in the studio dissolves to a February 3, 1968, photograph showing a lithe, well-groomed Elin Lindström standing outside of a black Volvo limousine talking with Swedish Premier Tage Erlander and U.S. Vice President Hubert Humphrey. The television camera moves-in for a close-up of the woman.

The frame freezes as Goransson says, "This photo is courtesy of noted Stockholm attorney Hans Belfrage." The shot then dissolves into the next news story, about the Vasa warship that sits on the shore alongside Stockholm's harbor.

◄ Chapter 37 ►

*Kalifornia Katherine Surprises Alec Ramsay in
Huron County's Jail in Bad Axe, Michigan, U.S.A.*

WEDNESDAY, NOVEMBER 6, 1996

It's Wednesday, November 6, 1996, and Alec Ramsay is quietly commemorating his slightly more than ten months locked up in the same hell hole of a cell. Ramsay's hair now is snow white, which says that lots of time has been served in the Huron County brig since he last enjoyed sitting down for an hour or so to get his monthly "tint 'n' trim" from his longtime Bloomfield Hills barber, Bill DeLosch.

Ramsay's hair looks chopped off, like maybe he did it himself ... without a mirror! Actually his haircut results from the bottom-feeder's skill of a local buzz-cutter who periodically makes a swing through the cell block with a pair of scissors, a large-toothed comb, a broom and a dustpan. Word around town is that this young man, otherwise apparently unemployable, is the bastard son of a former Bad Axe town manager.

The prisoner is lying in a half doze on his metal-framed bunk. A stack of yellow typewritten pages and handwritten notes lie haphazardly on the rusty grey metal table next to Ramsay's old L.C. Smith manual typewriter. Being able to concentrate on writing his story during the last nine months has kept Ramsay's mind busy and relatively fertile, and has obviously served to at least delay another jailhouse suicide in Bad Axe.

These days, an overabundance of prisoner suicides is making

Huron County's sheriff look bad. This sheriff worries about such things . . . unlike his predecessor, Sheriff Merritt McBride, who encouraged prisoner suicides because he said they were a sure fire cost-cutting measure.

It's been said that Sheriff McBride used money saved on prisoner rations to buy fancy silver saddles and other doo-dads for the handsome palomino that he rode in local parades throughout Michigan's Thumb.

Under Michigan state law, Huron County's sheriff can keep Alec Ramsay in his cell for twenty-three out of every twenty-four hours. It's that twenty-fourth hour of every single day that Ramsay treasures, because that's when he gets to take a warm shower in the common area shared with three other cells designed to hold the county's most incorrigible characters.

Although Alec Ramsay has never considered himself incorrigible, he readily admits to being just a tad opinionated. But Ramsay knows that his opinions no longer count for much!

Indeed, the county's legal machine continues to believe that Ramsay's mind is highly dangerous, corrupt and incorrigible! "They're all assholes, every last one," Ramsay mumbles to himself.

————

Somewhere along the tile-lined corridor, which reverberates with sound from all directions, Ramsay hears jackboots approaching. The jangling of a jailer's heavy keys is punctuated by the clanging and slamming of steel doors as they are opened and closed along the way.

A moment later, Ramsay recognizes the all-too-familiar squeaks from ancient hinges on the heavy door nearest his cell. Then he hears strange voices. *That's odd*, Ramsay thinks to himself. *It's between meals.* What he means is it's seldom that anybody comes to his end of the corridor.

Ramsay's nose tells him that it's Howard the Jailer, who seems proud of his world-class case of body odor. Indeed, Howard stops at Ramsay's cell door, enveloped in a cloud of body odor that's powerfully repugnant. Plus there's some sort of black crud smeared on the front of the grey uniform, which contrasts beautifully with the gold-colored swastika that hangs on a heavy chain around his neck.

Rather than try to make a joke about wanting to grab the chain and choke his jailer, Ramsay inquires, "Hey, my friend, what's the weather like today?"

Instead of uttering his usual one-word refrain—like "rain," "sun," "wind" or "snow"—Howard replies, "Somebody here to see ya, mate. You got pants on?

"Yeah, he's decent!" Howard says over his shoulder.

Ramsay mutters to himself, "What kind of comment is that?" On the other hand, he doesn't much care about anything that's being said by Howard or anybody. One gets to feeling and thinking that way after nearly a year of being tucked away with Huron County's *un-finest* in an essentially brain-dead environment.

The jailer steps back into the hallway and waves his hand. In a moment, two strangers step into the common area outside of Alec Ramsay's cell. Jesus Christ, is this *awkward time* or what?

One visitor is a rather short, but trim, fiftyish, dark-haired woman with a pretty face highlighted by a generous nose. She is accompanied by a tall, blond, blue-eyed young man. The pair couldn't look more dissimilar, although both exude a regal bearing and are elegantly dressed.

The woman is wearing a wide-brimmed dark blue hat and lightly tinted sunglasses. Her clothes are crisp blue linen with white trim, not the wash 'n wear preferred by most Huron County locals. Hereabouts, only blue-haired old ladies wear hats. And very few women even own sunglasses, possibly because the cost isn't covered by one federal support program or another.

The woman removes her sunglasses, revealing brown eyes, and Ramsay is suddenly blown away with emotion. He almost collapses into another world!

It's K.K.—Kalifornia Katherine—since 1957 his friend and pen pal from California. After all the years, she's still dazzling. And in her damp eyes Ramsay glimpses some of his own past.

The blond and blue-eyed young man is a different story. Ramsay never has seen pictures of Katherine's two sons, but this guy looks too Nordic to be Katherine's son! If he's not her son, then who the heck is he? And how come he's here?

Finally, first words are exchanged!

"Oh, my God," Ramsay gushes. "Hello, Katherine. What an unbelievable surprise. How embarrassing for you to see me here like this after so many years. Why, err . . . how the devil did you ever find me? Why are you here?"

Katherine demurs. "Later," she responds cryptically.

Searching for words, Ramsay says, "Now, which one of your sons is this, David or Phillip?" Katherine responds with a modest hug, and says, "Neither, dear Alexander." She has always called him Alexander. Just like Marie-Ann used to do, especially when she was angry!

"Now, you sit down right here, Alexander. We've both got something to say. And you need to listen carefully, so you can get up to speed on a few things."

Katherine remains standing. The young man sits down next to Ramsay on the jailhouse cot. He's sits flagpole-straight right on the cold metal edge.

———

Katherine begins. "First, let's see . . . now, how can I say this? Well, you should know that I'm aware of the mess you made regarding the settlement of your parents' estate. I probably would have suggested doing things a whole lot differently, but that's water over the dam.

"Second, your sister Wilma out in Boise has told me she forgives you for the pain and grief you brought upon her and other family members.

"In fact, I spoke with your sister just last week by phone, and it sounds like she plans never to set foot again in Michigan. I think she's genuinely scared of you. And she says that you've really spooked her former lawyer, too.

"Anyway, during this past summer your sister and her husband bought a big house near downtown Boise. They also have a new condominium in Sun Valley, although I think it's actually in Ketchum. You know, that's where my folks and I stayed when Daddy took us there in the early sixties to do research for another Putnam book entitled *Cher Papa*.

"But then, Alexander, you know all about *Cher Papa*! I remember that book was your idea . . . to take Daddy's surfer-girl character off the beach at Malibu and put her onto Sun Valley's ski slopes.

"Daddy always said it was a brilliant idea, although I'm afraid he was never particularly forthcoming when it came to paying compliments to others. I also think Daddy may have felt a little guilty about not giving you a little something out of the cash advance his publisher paid toward the manuscript."

Ramsay is speechless, still trying to fathom and to sort out what he's hearing.

The handsome young man sitting next to Ramsay still hasn't

uttered a sound. He's been silently sitting on the cot, staring intently at the prisoner next to him. Ramsay thinks to himself, *I wonder if the kid's mute and just can't talk.*

"Now Alexander, pay close attention to what I'm going to tell you." She places Ramsay's hand into hers. "It's regrettable that I never had a chance to meet Marie-Ann, although I feel I sort of knew her a little bit from those Christmas greeting cards our families exchanged for those many years. And, of course, I'm sure there's no way you could know about sweet Yehuda. It happened last spring. Cancer. So terribly sad for all of us."

Ramsay squeezes her hand. "Why, I'm so sorry, Katherine." In the old days, he almost always called her Katherine, particularly in serious moments.

She continues, "Dr. Murray Brennan at Sloan-Kettering did everything possible, and our family couldn't be more grateful to him and his team." Katherine pauses for a moment. "When your occasional phone calls stopped, Alexander, I had no easy way of telling you.

"So I called my friend, Silvie—the one who complains about living in the smallest house on Arlington Road in Birmingham, and whose husband is with the FBI in Detroit. I asked her to do some sniffing around for me, and that's when I found out about Marie-Ann's leaving. And then I started to learn bit-by-bit about the sticky predicament involving your sister, the farm and all.

"I tried to recall some of what you had told me in old letters about your Swedish acquaintance, Elin Lindström. God, that goes all the way back to your Manhattan and D.C. days in the '60s. For some peculiar reason—and I wasn't exactly sure why at the time—I decided to try and contact Elin. Guess maybe I had too much time on my hands.

"I didn't even know where to start because so many years had passed. You know how it is. Everything changes. Names and addresses change; even countries, too. And I really knew very little about Sweden except that Stockholm is on the east coast, and Gothenburg and Marstrand Island are on the west coast.

"And of course I had seen some Swedish films because Ingmar Bergmann, Max von Sydow and a few others were international theatrical clients represented by Daddy's brother, Paul. Anyway, I came across the name of Elin's half-brother in one of your old letters. It was George . . . hmmm . . . George Grant!

"You once wrote me about meeting him when you had dinner at Grant's Taverna on Strandvägen in Stockholm. So I called the Swedish Consul's office in Los Angeles, and they told me that Grant's Taverna was long gone, and by now had probably been replaced along the Strand by yet another big office building.

"That sort of reminded me of when your friends, Keith and Lucille Lloyd, literally moved their old mission-style house. It's the one where you rented a room in the late '50s . . . at 15007 Ventura Boulevard, right across from the Sherman Oaks Theatre. I remember watching when it was being moved, perched atop dozens of wheels, to the neighborhood just north of Moorpark.

"The hole in the ground left on Ventura became one more Plain-Jane savings & loan building. On the plus side, I guess the Lloyds made lots of money on the deal, which helped them to buy their dream home in Ojai, where you once took me for a visit.

"Shush, Alexander," said Katherine, sensing that he was about to say something! "Now you let me finish. It'll just take another minute.

"Anyway, I then visited the Swedish Consul's office in Los Angeles and spent an entire afternoon leafing through a stack of Swedish telephone books. Finally, I found a George Grant living west of Stockholm, near a town called Eskilstuna. See there,

Alexander, aren't you proud that I'm serious about trying to pronounce some Swedish place names."

She continues, "I can assure you that Mr. Grant was more than a little puzzled when I telephoned him all the way from California. And he was really surprised—no, I'd say *shocked* is a better word— when I asked about his sister Elin.

"At first, I thought he was a little rude. I now know he was just naturally a bit standoffish—which I understand is an integral part of the Swedish psyche.

"Because I didn't want George to hang up the phone on me, I quickly told him I was flying to Stockholm the following week and would be honored to meet him and his wife, and take them to dinner at a little restaurant I'd heard about in Stockholm's Old Town.

"And, just like that, he said, 'okay.' What I didn't know was that the old Urgamlaskällaren Restaurant is now called Diana. It's named after the goddess of hunting, not the British princess, and apparently it's been at the same Brunnsgränd 2 address since the early 1970s.

"What a fabulous place it is! Simply exquisite. And the split curved stairway going downstairs is uniquely spectacular!

"When George and Susanna received me in their home last month, and before we drove into Stockholm for dinner, they introduced me to Erik here who was visiting them from West Sweden. So I asked if Erik would like to join us for dinner."

While Ramsay struggled to put a sentence together, Katherine continued, "It turns out that Erik was raised in the Grant household after his mother suffered a mental breakdown in the 1970s. She was hospitalized pretty much through the late 1980s, and finally died in 1989. Although I'm not 100 percent sure, I think it was by her own hand. I don't know any details." From his teary eyes, it was clear that young Erik understood what was being said.

Alexander Ramsay can't contain himself any longer, and reaches for an old tee-shirt lying on the pillow. He swabs both eyes.

Katherine pauses for a moment, before continuing her story. "George told me that Erik's mother was Elin Lindström. And on Erik's birth certificate, Elin listed "Alexander W. Ramsay" as Erik's father!"

Ramsay's face drains, and his body slumps even deeper onto the cot.

Young Erik and Alec Ramsay stare at each other for a nano-second before springing up from the jail cell cot and into each other's arms. They grab each other, kissing and hugging and crying. Both are bawling out loud, unashamedly.

Katherine remains calm while reaching into her purse. There's a bright white flash as Katherine snaps a photo of Erik and his dad, with tears streaming down their cheeks.

Rather gingerly, and then almost in unison, Katherine and Erik glance at each other for a moment before turning to ask Ramsay, "Well, Alexander—errr, Dad—are you ready for a change of scenery?"

His mind is churning as he thinks to himself, *They're kidding! How?*

The fact is, he's bone-tired from all the shit that's been going on in his life during the past few years, including having so many friends and family members die during a short span of time.

For the first time in ten months, Ramsay admits, "Hell, yeah, I'm ready to get outta here. Like in a heartbeat! But I don't know how."

And he really does want out. Like right now! It's high time for a new beginning. No more questions to be asked; no more answers to be sought.

The fifty-six-year-old woman standing in front of Ramsay finally breaks into tears of her own. "Alexander, I've always loved you, too . . . and, yes, maybe all of us deserve a chance to jump-start our lives . . . maybe even together." The three embrace, even if a little clumsily.

Katherine explains, manner-of-factly, that "All the papers have been signed for your release from this joint." She quickly adds, "So, let's gather up only what you really need and get out of here before somebody downstairs changes his mind."

Ramsay turns toward Howard the Jailer, who has been standing patiently a few steps down the corridor. "Please tell the good sheriff that my old typewriter is all his. If he's changed his mind since February and no longer wants it, ask him to please donate it to the Huron County Historical Society. They already have a large brown-grey Royal manual that my folks gave them back in the early 1980s.

"Tell everyone that this old typewriter's still got lots of loving miles left on it. Just like me!"

Erik finally speaks up, in a British-tinged accent, probably taught to him in a Swedish grammar school by a teacher trained to speak British-tinged English. "Hurry, Papa. Let's go."

"Oh my God, Katherine, do you hear that? *My son's first words!*" The threesome are wearing grins and tears.

With a sense of renewal and the unbeatable combination of gleaming smiles, brisk steps and tear-stained faces, they walk out of the jailhouse door—arm-in-arm-in-arm—and into the clear, crisp November afternoon sunlight.

Parked down the street, Alex Ramsay recognizes an old friend. It's Elin's red 1968 Camaro convertible, with the white ragtop folded down. Ramsay knows that Erik's mother, Elin—the real *Ragtop Doll*—would be so proud!

So what if a few townie tongues may be wagging at the three-person tableau inexplicably unfolding before them! But who really cares? Certainly not Alexander Ramsay. For him, the incredible thing is that Erik's mother's old car still lives.

Indeed, it's the same bright red Camaro that Horatio had given to Erik's momma, Elin Lindström, in late 1967. And now the car will belong to Erik!

Remembering Harry Treleavan's dark admonition to him in 1968, Ramsay had made a promise to Elin on that fateful day in mid-May 1968. It was a rainy afternoon at the Westchester County Airport, just north of Manhattan, as Elin prepared to depart for Sweden aboard Gil Silverman's private airplane.

Alec promised Elin that he would arrange to keep her car safely stored and maintained until she called for it. Probably it would be kept in a garage behind one of the several homes in Amagansett that Harry Treleavan owned for investment purposes. Elin promised to let Ramsay know when she had decided what to do with her car.

Elin's options included having the Camaro sold in the United States, or perhaps it would be shipped to Sweden aboard the S.S. *Saab*. The huge boat arrived every two weeks at the port of New Haven, Connecticut, loaded with brand-new Saab cars destined for dealerships in New England and a few scattered parts of the United States where the still-quirky Saab brand was gaining popularity among sophisticated car enthusiasts.

The boat almost always returned to Göteborg empty. The exceptions were when one or another of the young bucks working at Detroit's Swedish Trade Office would try to make a few extra dollars by shipping a muscle car to Sweden aboard the boat. Among friends of Sweden's young King Carl XVI Gustaf—known in Detroit as FOKs [friends of the King]—there was a ready market for hot new Pontiac Firebirds, Chevy Camaros and Ford Mustangs.

Happily for all, Bob Sinclair, President and CEO of Saab USA, was always most accommodating when it came to servicing the FOKs and Stig Björkman's boys at Detroit's Swedish Trade Office!

Once she had returned to Sweden, Elin appeared to be confused about all sorts of things. She seemed unable to sort out and make firm decisions about even the simplest, most basic of matters. Her somewhat impaired mental state rapidly pushed her downhill toward oblivion.

After her son's birth in Uddevalla Hospital, Elin dropped completely out of sight and seemingly cut herself off from the world. Ramsay would never again be in touch with her.

In the aftermath of the 1968 election, Ramsay married Marie-Ann Eklund. The newlyweds turned down Bob Haldeman's invitation to move to Washington, D.C., opting instead for a new position with an advertising agency in Ramsay's home state of Michigan. It was there that they started a family that within six years grew to include three daughters and a lovable mutt named Lucifer Seymour. Each girl was a gifted student and extremely curious about life beyond Michigan, traits that continue to this day.

Once a year, for almost thirty years, Ramsay mailed a six-hundred-dollar check to Harry Treleavan's home in Amagansett, near the tip of New York's Long Island. Always attached was a handwritten note that extended season's greetings to Harry and his family, and expressed hope that "this will be the year I can arrange to take the Camaro off your hands."

Although Ramsay always mailed a copy of his letter to Elin's last known address on Marstrand, he never heard from her. And only once, in the late 1970s, did he take some time to visit Harry in beautiful Amagansett on the south shore of easternmost Long Island.

"You know, *my son*. . . . " Oh, those two words, *'my son,'* feel so wonderful twirling off Ramsay's tongue. He starts again. "You know, Erik, you would have loved your mother's friend, Hubert Humphrey, too. He was a very special gentleman, with a spirit that soared so high and a heart so much bigger and more generous than people today can ever know or imagine.

"Even the most cantankerous of Vice President Humphrey's political opponents agreed that the logic and verbosity that flowed constantly from his 'magic mouth' was more than matched by his graciousness, keen intellect, photographic memory, honesty and social consciousness."

Erik listens intently, trying to fathom precisely what it is his dad is saying.

Ramsay continues, "Vice President Humphrey was maybe the brightest man I've ever known. He had an ability to articulate a wonderful, enlightened vision for America, for your own country of Sweden, the Middle East and the entire world.

"The thing is, your mother's special friend was probably ten or fifteen years ahead of everyone else. And sometimes that can make lesser people uncomfortable.

"One of my deepest regrets is that Hubert Humphrey wasn't elected U.S. president in 1968. He would have been a truly great president for all the people! And there can be little doubt that today's world would be much better than it is."

They reach the Chevy Camaro, parked beside the curb, and Ramsay tosses in his small brown bag—containing a few personal items, including three small photos with dried toothpaste on the back, and a thick yellow manuscript—onto the back seat of the open convertible.

Erik climbs into the driver's seat, while his dad holds open the passenger door for Katherine. Despite her protestation, he insists that she should sit in the front seat next to young Erik.

Ramsay gently closes the Camaro's heavy passenger-side door, and then vaults into the back seat! "By God, these old bones still have it," he shouts. Indeed, Alec Ramsay is feeling pretty darn special, and maybe even a little too frisky for an old fart.

Across Bad Axe's Huron Street, an elderly couple walks slowly toward their home, each one lugging a cloth grocery bag. They glance toward the red car parked in front of the courthouse, but pay no particular attention to the convertible with its top down in November.

Erik ignites the engine and guns the small-block V-8 with its dual carbs and twin pipes. The 1968 red Chevrolet Camaro RS/ SS convertible pulls slowly away from the curb and rumbles west on Huron until it can turn left just short of Murphy's Bakery.

After all these years, the Doll's ragtop is finally going home to Sweden, where it belongs. It'll cost maybe four hundred dollars to ship it from New Haven to Göteborg aboard the S.S. *Saab*, thanks to two of Ramsay's friends at General Motors, Bob Hendry and Bo Andersson.

Ramsay mutters absentmindedly, "Finally, all of us are going back to Sweden . . . and we're going together. I swear, if I ever return to Bad Axe and Huron County, it'll be as ashes in an urn."

He quietly reflects to himself, *Somebody—maybe my three daughters and their new half-brother—can plant my ashes in the ground next to the generations of Ramsays and Richmonds already buried in the family plot next to the township hall, two miles north of town.*

On second thought, it'll be a lot simpler and probably more fun for every-one to simply sprinkle my remains onto the waters of the Gulf Stream that arcs across the Atlantic all the way from the Gulf of Mexico to the Skägerrak. It's the same Gulf Stream that splashes ashore at young Erik's small farm on the West Coast island of Skaftö, only two kilometers from Fiskebäckskil.

That's precisely what we did when Marie-Ann's papa died back in the 1970s.

How much pleasure I hope and expect my friends and family shall have when I die! thinks Alec to himself.

With proper planning, my demise will happen during the months of July or August, so that folks can enjoy a real Swedish celebration on the sun-drenched meadow next to the sea. There'll be a fabulous smörgåsbord. And plenty of icy cold aquavit, beer and Swedish Punch to punctuate the speeches, laughter, singing and dancing around the huge summer bonfire on the rocks by the shore.

Damn, sounds like I'll be missing one mighty fine party!

◄ Epilogue ►

*Christmas Eve Day in West Sweden's
Picturesque Coastal Village of Fiskebäckskil*

MONDAY, DECEMBER 24, 2003

So much has happened since that afternoon in November, 1996, when Katherine and young Erik rescued me, Alec Ramsay, from that jail cell in Michigan.

While we did visit Sweden later that same month, maybe not surprisingly the old magic just wasn't there for Katherine and me. We enjoyed our visit with the Grants, Elin's half-brother and his wife in Eskilstuna. And, best of all, we spent a few days with Erik at his small farm on Skaftö island, not far from Uddevalla.

We assiduously tried to avoid running into any of Marie-Ann's relatives who lived in the area, partly to spare all of us embarrassment while I was still working out some old issues that had plagued my marriage.

We almost succeeded, except for that one afternoon when I ran into Marie-Ann's younger sister, Cilla, while buying food at Tempo Skaftöhallen in Fiskebäckskil. Fortunately, neither Katherine nor Erik was with me.

It didn't take too long for Sweden's storied winter darkness to persuade Katherine that sunny southern California was where she really belonged. Malibu and its environs were her heritage and home, and also close by to where her two sons lived. She still owned two homes in Pacific Palisades, one a rental property that provided her with a comfortable income.

While in Sweden, Katherine began toying with the idea of trying to work out a deal whereby her father's estate would authorize republishing some of Dr. Kohner's better-known books, starting with the classic *Gidget*, a thinly-disguised novel based on Katherine's early surfing experiences at Malibu, which was first published in 1957 by Bantam through arrangement with G.P. Putnam's Sons.

I recall that the original paperback version cost twenty-five cents in the United States, and served as a cross-promotion for Columbia Pictures' sparkling version of *Gidget* in 1959 starring Sandra Dee and James Darren. Last I checked, the film still is available on cassette or DVD at Blockbuster, and is probably in many local libraries along with the two sequels, *Gidget Goes Hawaiian* and *Gidget Goes To Rome*.

In fact, Bantam did reissue *Gidget* as a paperback in early 2001—with a wonderful foreword by Katherine—and I hear that it's selling well. I hope that plans are in the works to reissue some of her father's other excellent books, such as *Kiki of Montparnasse*, *The Magician of Sunset Boulevard* and *Hanna and Walter*.

Indeed, Katherine's initiatives continue to bear fruit and provide pleasure and wonderful memories for *Gidget* fans everywhere.

———

Swedes around the world celebrate the Christmas holiday in the same manner year after year—and this year will be no different.

It's Christmas Eve day; Marie-Ann and I have gathered our extended multi-national family around us at our new waterfront home overlooking the harbor at Fiskebäckskil. The best news of all is that Marie-Ann and I are happily reconciled, and now enjoy some of the best days of our long married life together.

Seated around the colorful and festive holiday table are Marie-Ann, myself, our three daughters and Erik; Marie-Ann's ninety-one-year-old mother, Karin; and Marie-Ann's younger sister, her two brothers and their respective families.

Also there are the bright and lively babies recently born to Malin and Sara. Seated in high-chairs are the older grandchildren. Their mothers hold the newborns in their arms. And it is to each of these youngsters, plus Erik and his beloved mother, Elin—the authentic Ragtop Doll—that this story is dedicated.

The main table and a side table are spread with a broad variety of Swedish dishes, similar to those served to Erik's mother, Elin, and her American vice-presidential consort at the restaurant in Stockholm's Old Town on February 3, 1968.

Two special holiday guests visiting from the United States are Dick and Diana Wise, old friends and neighbors from Michigan. The Wises have participated in almost every Swedish Christmas Eve dinner celebration that Marie-Ann and our family have hosted over the years in our Bloomfield Hills, Michigan home.

If memory is correct, the Wises missed only two Christmases . . . once when our family visited the Caribbean islands of St. Kitts & Nevis, and then that painful year when Marie-Ann and I were estranged.

Because the Wises have met most of our Swedish relatives at one time or another in the United States, this Christmas holiday in Sweden is sort of like Old Home Week for them. Not only does everyone know each other, they genuinely like each other. Couldn't be more perfect!

As happens at any Swedish gathering—whether at the Ramsays' table or elsewhere—speeches and toasts are encouraged. In fact, they're a requisite part of the Swedish dining experience. And the more folks who stand up and speak, the merrier!

After I start things off—on behalf of Marie-Ann and me—by welcoming everyone to our Christmas table, I thank everyone for making the effort to attend.

Except for Marie-Ann's sister, Cilla, who lives only a short walk away from our waterside home, young Erik lives the closest. His six-and-half-hectare farm—that's about thirteen acres in size—borders the big water less than two kilometers from Fiskebäckskil. It's the anchor to which he happily returns whenever he's not playing golf on the European Tour.

———

In a large old barn on Erik's farm is his mother's storied and historic 1968 Chevrolet Camaro convertible. The car is raised off the barn floor to preserve the red-rimmed tires. Two or three times a year, Erik has Arne Polsson, a mechanic friend from nearby Östersidan, take the Camaro off of the blocks and check all the fluids and systems. Arne then cranks up the powerful 350 small-block V-8 engine and proudly drives three or four times around the island.

Many of the wealthy summer residents who reside in Fiskebäckskil and other areas on the island of Skaftö have by now heard the story about Erik's car. Occasionally one of them asks Erik how much cash he would like for his car. Erik always smiles politely and quietly says that his classic Chevy isn't for sale.

Most of these folks don't really believe Erik because they are so used to being able to afford and acquire anything that comes within their sight. After all, these are powerful and persistent Swedish business and government executives, accustomed to almost always having their way.

Folks who own homes in Fiskebäckskil typically rank among the highest-profile business, government, and cultural thought leaders in Sweden. At their cocktail parties they sometimes speculate as to which among them will eventually persuade Erik to sell them his most treasured possession. Indeed, several area residents already own classic Cadillac cars and are members of Sweden's Cadillac Owners Club, the world's largest.

If Erik was to ever seriously consider selling his car, it might well be to the Minneapolis-based heir and daughter of Kurt-Visby Rädisson. Marilyn Rädisson knows all about Erik's mother and her close association with her dad's close friend, the former U.S. vice president from Minnesota.

Marilyn's father had long ago shared with her what he knew about the tryst aboard his yacht one wintry February night long ago in Stockholm's harbor. But Marilyn doesn't know the whole story, and probably never will.

———

Following three or four hours of eating, laughing, swapping stories, speeches, frequent *skoaling* and general carrying on at the Christmas table, Alec Ramsay once again rises from his chair and—to get everyone's attention—taps his small Swedish crystal aquavit glass with a silver teaspoon.

But before he can squeeze out the first word, daughter Anika—who has been serving throughout the meal as a story-teller and laugh fomenter—pre-empts her dad.

"Sit down, Papa," she says. "It's my turn!"

Anika proceeds to thank her parents for bringing together family and friends on this special occasion. She offers special thanks to her mother and the Swedish relatives for teaching her, Sara and Malin to appreciate and actively celebrate their special Swedish heritage and language. Everyone applauds by snapping their fingers.

Because Anika usually is a tough act to follow, Alec decides to recast his remarks to avoid repetition. Somewhat inexplicably, he comments on the similarities he has observed between his favorite seacoast towns in Sweden, the United States and Morocco. He says they are the fishing villages of Fiskebäckskil on Sweden's West Coast, Camden in Maine along America's East Coast, and Essaouira on Morocco's Atlantic coast. All three communities grew in prosperity and greatness, at various times in history, based on a salt water fishing economy.

Ramsay then draws some parallels and distinctions between the national governments in Sweden, the United States and Morocco. Perhaps the most surprising factoid he reveals is that Morocco was the very first country to recognize the new country of America after it was founded in the year 1776.

He says, "This helps explain why America and Morocco have always supported each other's economic, political and cultural interests. And thus it can be argued that as Morocco goes, so goes America. And Sweden, too, for that matter."

In wrapping up his remarks, Alex alludes to a few highlights in his life. His marriage to Marie-Ann and the birth of their three daughters certainly top the pyramid.

But the moment quickly is becoming uncomfortable for Marie-Ann and the girls, who seem to realize, almost simultaneously, that Alec's speech is practically identical to one they remember Alec's cancer-ridden father delivering at a Thanksgiving Day dinner on the Michigan family farm just one day before blowing out his brains with a long rifle in the laundry room.

Sensing the growing level of unease around the table, Alec does a verbal one-eighty. He switches direction by saying he certainly looks forward to many more productive years of writing books, creating his unique and sought-after circular abstract oil paintings, and, best of all, helping and watching his grandchildren grow up in the United States, Morocco and Sweden as productive citizens of the world.

Alec speaks about how delighted he is to see Marie-Ann so contented and fulfilled, knowing that she has the freedom to do whatever she wishes, whenever and wherever she wishes. He smiles when he suggests that some of Marie-Ann's happiness may be related to the almost one ton of paper and stuff that he tossed out when they decided to scale down their home in Michigan.

He laughingly recalls how he'd heard that the Bloomfield Hills' Waste Management trash-collection team later tried to insert a clause in a new union contract, whereby they would receive an extra paid vacation day each year on the anniversary of the day Ramsay's almost-one-ton pile of trash was picked up at the curb. Admittedly, that sounds a little over the top!

Alec wraps up his remarks with a quotation by his favorite American politician, which he'd once shared with Erik's mother, Elin. *"In real life, unlike in Shakespeare, the sweetness of the rose depends upon the name it bears. Things are not only what they are. They are, in very important respects, what they seem to be."*

Across the table, Alec notices that young Erik's eyes are tearing, although his lips were smiling.

With that, Ramsay says, "Damn, this has been a mighty fine party. I'm truly blessed with family and friends.

"But having said that," he continues, "I'm no less secular than before! All I'm trying to say is that you're all invited back to Fiskebäckskil one year from today. Same time, same place. Or please come back and see us sooner if you can. Now, why don't we see what might be under the holiday tree for the grandkids. Okay?"

"But first, how about one more skål for all of us around the table. And, perhaps even more important, a skål for all of those who couldn't be with us today!"

"SKÅL!" was shouted in unison by all.

◄ Postscript ►

Where Have All the Players Gone?

Following the 1968 U.S. presidential election, several of Alec Ramsay's associates at J. Walter Thompson Company went to Washington and worked for the Nixon administration. Dwight Chapin signed on as Nixon's appointments secretary. Ron Ziegler became Nixon's press secretary and assistant to the president, while Bob Haldeman was asked to be President Nixon's all-powerful White House chief-of-staff.

Several other JWTers left the advertising business to serve in a variety of roles in the Nixon administration and important federal agencies, including Voice of America.

For the most part, the former JWTers were forced out of government in the aftermath of the late-night June 17, 1972 Watergate break-in fiasco, which had been foretold by Attorney General John Mitchell in his final team meeting at Nixon's Park Avenue campaign headquarters on Saturday afternoon, November 2, 1968.

Harry Treleavan—who never much enjoyed working with John Mitchell, Frank Shakesphere and Bob Haldeman—left JWT after the 1968 election to build a highly-successful political-consulting firm. With two winning political campaigns under his belt—one in 1966 for Texas' newly minted U.S. Congressman, George Herbert Walker Bush, and another for Richard Nixon in 1968—Treleavan decided to work only for Republican candidates who could meet his stringent requirements regarding honesty, morality and financial integrity.

For fun and additional profit, Treleavan continued to buy up older homes on the southeasternmost part of Long Island. He fixed up each one and then rented them—mostly to rich Manhattanites who wanted to escape the city on weekends. At one point, Treleavan and his family owned nineteen or twenty homes in and around Amagansett.

Richard Milhaus Nixon served as U.S. President between January 20, 1969, and that fateful day in 1974 when he was replaced by Michigan congressman and Speaker of the U.S. House of Representatives, Gerald R. Ford. Indeed, Nixon had finally been toppled by the infamous Watergate affair.

Elin Lindström returned to Sweden during 1968 and gave birth to her son, Erik, in early November. She chose to live a lonely, rather uneven life on Sweden's West Coast. Ultimately, Elin committed suicide, while nearby her neighbors sang and danced around a traditional flower-bedecked Swedish midsummer pole on an otherwise perfect June afternoon. Ironically, her body was autopsied at the same Uddevalla hospital where she had given birth to Erik many years earlier.

The distinguished Washington, D.C., lawyer, Andrew Gallagher Ryan, was buried with full military honors in Arlington Cemetery, after four decades as an ultimate Washington insider. Following a Catholic service in Fort Myer's main chapel, the massive mahogany casket containing Ryan's body was carried to the gravesite aboard the same horse-drawn black caisson that a few sad years earlier had borne JFK's shattered remains.

Mohammad Al-Wahid, whose son had failed to kill Vice President Humphrey in Stockholm on February 1, 1968, is credited with commissioning Robert F. Kennedy's assassination in Los Angeles during the long, deadly spring of 1968.

Now an old man living quietly on a green hilltop overlooking Damascus, Al-Wahid long ago foresworn the strategy of terrorism-as-a-weapon. Even so, he remains convinced that in each year since 1947 America's powerful Jewish lobby has used massive infusions of money to influence powerful members of the U.S. Congress —plus every American president since Harry S. Truman —to bankroll Zionist interests, always to Palestine's detriment, and to spawn an Israeli military machine whose firepower is second only to America's and whose intelligence network is superior to America's!

The now secular Al-Wahid fervently believes that ultra-conservative religious leaders, politicians and other freaks in America who scheme and cooperate under the cloak of Christianity and God are just as dangerous to world peace as any of the rabid, venom-spewing and oft-lethal religious conservatives who try to exert mind control over adherents to Islam, Judaism, Hinduism, Buddhism and most other world religions.

Swedish lawyer Hans Belfrage is world renowned for his negotiating skills. Belfrage, his wife and daughter lived in London for twenty years before returning to live in the Belfrage ancestral home outside of Stockholm. He continues as a senior partner in Sweden's blue-chip law firm, Vinge.

The late Kurt-Visby Rädisson's daughter, Marilyn, has success-fully used her intelligence and style to continue her father's mission of building one of the world's largest private fortunes. Her Minneapolis-based, service-oriented holding company is multi-national and encompasses hotels, restaurants, cruise lines and travel agencies.

As U.S. Vice President Hubert Humphrey once predicted to Elin Lindström, the following words are immodestly carved on Rädisson's mammoth Swedish granite tombstone in a suburban

Minneapolis cemetery: "Here rests the richest Swedish-American of them all."

Kalifornia Katherine, the real-life surfer girl named Gidget, is a living icon who continues to reside in the Los Angeles area. She's exceedingly proud and grateful that the popular stories and movies written during the '40s, '50s and '60s by her immigrant father, Dr. Frederick Kohner, continue to set a positive tone for youth culture in America and around the world.

Alec Ramsay declined Bob Haldeman's invitation to join President Nixon's White House communications staff. After being married in All Saints Episcopal Church on East 60th Street in Manhattan, Marie-Ann and Alec moved to Bloomfield Hills, Michigan, so they could raise and educate their family far from the glitz, gridlock and media-driven frenzy that are hallmarks of life in Manhattan and Washington, D.C.

After his narrow defeat by Richard Nixon in 1968, former U.S. Vice President Hubert Humphrey returned to Minnesota where he taught for a few years at Macalester College and the University of Minnesota.

Time often has a way of healing political wounds, and the fine people of Minnesota once again elected Humphrey to represent them in the U.S. Senate. Senate Democratic leaders in Washington then awarded Senator Humphrey the seniority he enjoyed before being elected U.S. vice president in November 1964 under President Lyndon Baines Johnson.